GUMBO YAYA EXIT

THE BIG UNEASY
BOOK 10

PAULINE BAIRD JONES

ABOUT GUMBO YA-YA EXIT

In New Orleans, secrets don't stay buried—and neither do old, cold sins...

Madeline Baker thrives on order. By day, she runs the front desk at Baker Boys Investigations; by night, she's mystery author S.C. Fitz-Dankworthington—her best-kept secret. She's got a deadline looming and no time for danger or romance.

Then Quinn Ellery walks in, seeking her alter ego. His neighbor—another S.C. Fitz-Dankworthington—has been murdered, and he's convinced it's no coincidence. Soon after, his grandmother ropes Maddie into solving a 60-year-old killing—until someone tries to blow Gammie up and nearly takes them out instead.

Caught in a deadly web of family lies and long-buried truths, Maddie and Quinn race to unravel the past before it buries them too. In the Big Uneasy, murder and mayhem simmer with romance, gumbo, and secrets too close to home. Get your copy now to return to the Big Easy with the Bakers!

1

Madeline Baker let herself into the offices of *Baker Boys Investigations*—the "s" added when her brother Frank joined forces with her other brother Gideon.

She flipped the light switch with her elbow and then set her purse and laptop bag on the ridiculously small reception desk. There was a chair behind the desk, but nothing else. No plants, no pictures on the walls, not even a clock or a file cabinet. There just wasn't room.

The cost-per-square-foot suited Gideon's budget, a moving target according to her brother.

Gideon's office did have a file cabinet, though he didn't use it for files. The top of it sported a small fridge for cold drinks and the drawers were his snack pantry and a "closet," where he kept a change of clothes.

Frank, who now used the opposite office, wasn't fond of the vaguely Sam Spade look, but admitted it was an uphill battle both esthetically and financially. His IKEA desk was nice, but it looked a bit forlorn in the setting and the framed, postmodern print kept getting knocked off the wall every time Frank forgot to be careful when he moved around his desk.

The tiny vase with a single, artificial rose was nice. Maddie wasn't sure how long it would last because Frank's laptop upgrade looked ready to edge it out.

Her own small, battered desk did have room for her laptop and a cold drink if she was careful. Two drawers impinged into her leg space, but she needed someplace to put her purse and snacks. At least she didn't have to worry about phones and such taking up space. The room might be Sam Spade retro, but the tech was twenty-first century.

This didn't stop her from feeling vaguely 50s Della Street. She blamed this on Gideon. She couldn't prove it, but she suspected he saw himself as a modern version of Perry Mason's PI sidekick, Paul Drake.

And yes, she knew that Della had been Perry's secretary, but that didn't change how she felt when she answered a call or greeted a possible client. She'd swear she channeled Della at those moments. She sure as heck wasn't going to channel the snotty receptionist at the firm where she used to work.

If any of her former colleagues could see her now, they'd be shocked and possibly dismayed by her "come down."

Maddie, however, was quite happy to have made what she considered a lateral career move. The fact that very few people —including most of her family—hadn't heard about the move was about privacy while she regrouped, not about being embarrassed at being wrong about her legal career.

She hated being "I told you so'd" as much as the next person.

She'd resigned, not been fired. It had taken her about two days to process the face that she wasn't cut out to be a law firm type lawyer. That did not mean she wanted to go into criminal law, so that ruled out becoming either a public defender or a prosecutor.

It wasn't that she hated criminal law, but as the youngest of thirteen siblings who had mostly found some kind of law abiding or enforcing way to make a living, she wanted to do, and be, different—without becoming a criminal, of course. She'd wanted to forge her own path with a comfortable distance between her and the Baker legacy.

Well, she'd got it. She glanced around the small space. At least she wasn't paying her brothers rent for it, at least not really. She'd offered to be their receptionist in exchange for using it for a place to put her laptop that wasn't her apartment with a room-mate inclined to ask questions if she never saw her go to work.

Both brothers had been surprised when Maddie asked if she could use their outer office in exchange for being their recep-tionist.

"Did you get laid off?" Gideon's question had been asked without judgement.

"No," she said.

"Sure," he'd responded.

The only other thing Frank had said was, "Good."

It always amused her, the things that guys were curious about and the things they weren't. Her sisters would have been all over her with questions. But if a guy loomed up in her life? Then they got all up in her grill, her brothers most of all. Men really were an alien species.

None of her siblings had been thrilled when she'd opted for a law career, though some of them had found her legal advice useful. Her dad, a retired cop, had been vocally and persistently not thrilled. He recognized the need for lawyers and deplored the necessity.

She had no idea what her brothers thought she would use the office space for, but they hadn't hesitated to claim her as an on-staff legal advisor for their clients. A few of them had even paid her for her legal services.

So far, to her immense surprise, no one but Gideon and Frank had noticed she wasn't working at the firm that had hired her after graduation.

She didn't want to out herself until she collected a few more author clients. Helen had sent her two clients, but publishing money was like a slow bleed, so it helped to be on the spot for Gideon and Frank and pick up some extra cash. And she loved being out of the firm, even if the surroundings were a definite downgrade.

Three clients wouldn't pay her bills, of course. So, it was a good thing she'd added a new income stream before handing in her resignation.

At some point, she'd have to come clean about that, too.

She stowed her purse in the drawer with the lock, freed her laptop from the bag, and woke it up.

On the laptop, she had what she called her Della setup, an app that let her take and make calls for her brothers, and her own dedicated business line.

It was early, it was quiet, and she might be able to get some time for her own side hustle before her brothers arrived. But before she could open that file, an alert popped up.

She had several special ones that helped her keep track of outside events that might impact her or her clients.

This particular alert surprised her. It was not one she'd expected to ever get.

"Mysterious Death of Local Hermit"

She frowned and clicked the link. The article was from *The Plonkville Daily,* a small-town newspaper. It had, apparently, taken a few days to hit the search engines because the article was a couple of days old and scant on details.

Local hermit, Solice Circuit Fitz-Dankworthington was found dead early Friday morning. Police are investigating.

The implication that there was a police force would have

normally made her smile. She'd been to Plonkville once. Its "force" consisted of a chief and a deputy—both who had other jobs to make ends meet. There was a mayor who had expressed conventional sorrow at the loss.

And that was it.

The next alert had more detail—troubling detail.

Bestselling Author Found Dead in Home?

Was the recently deceased hermit actually the bestselling author, S. C. Fitz-Dankworthington?

Maddie managed to find space for both elbows to rest on either side of her laptop. Well, that explained the alert.

A call came through her laptop set up, this for her own business. The number was unknown. She hesitated. She usually didn't answer unknown calls on this particular number, but... she glanced at the headline and then took the call.

She heard a male voice identifying himself as a police officer and asking if he was speaking to M. Baker, literary agent for Mr. Fitz-Dankworthington.

His tone sounded pained, as if saying the name actually hurt and her lips twitched.

"Literary attorney," Maddie corrected, automatically. Her first instinct had been to stall and play assistant to herself, but probably not a good idea to do to an officer of the law. If he was who he said he was? It's not like she could check his ID while they were on the phone.

Authors had tried all kinds of dodges to get in touch with her since she'd hung up her virtual shingle as a literary attorney.

A hint of impatience entered the voice. "You're hard to track down, ma'am."

"Yes." She didn't apologize. She'd done it on purpose, and it was nice to know it had worked so well. With a family like hers, keeping your head down was both a genetic instinct and an imperative if one had secrets.

"I'm surprised you haven't been in touch," the voice pressed on, the annoyance factor rising. "Since your client is dead."

Maddie took a calming breath.

"Your Mr. Fitz-Dankworthington isn't my client," she said. "My client doesn't reside in Plonkville."

She was sure she felt him thinking through the connection.

"I just saw the news," she added, in case he wondered how she knew about Plonkville. Both that name, and the name of the victim would engender some interest. It might even make a few comedy monologues, so she needed to nip the connection in the bud right now.

"You're telling me there are *two* Solice Circuit Fitz-Dankworthingtons?" He didn't try to hide his skepticism.

"I don't know about that. My client's name isn't Solice Circuit Fitz-Dankworthington." She heard him inhale.

"And what is your client's name?"

"S. C. Fitz-Dankworthington."

"What—"

"That is the name on the contracts," Maddie broke in. "But his address isn't in Plonkville."

A heavy breathing silence followed this. "Quite a coincidence."

"Indeed."

"He didn't consider using a pseudonym?"

"Some authors want their name on the covers of their books," she pointed out.

"It's..."

"His editor wasn't that thrilled either," Maddie offered.

"So, your author has absolutely no connection to my," he hesitated, "victim?"

"Not as far as I am aware," she said.

"They have to be related with that last name."

He was persistent, she'd give him credit for that.

"I would expect that information to be found among your," she hesitated as well because the name was a mouthful, "victim's papers?"

Now a frown creased her brows. Had this Fitz-Dankworthington's death been natural? *Police are investigating.*

"I would like to speak to your client."

"I can relay your request to my client," she said.

"I'd like to call him."

"I would need his permission to give you his phone number," Maddie said. "I'm afraid he is very reclusive and would need to know why you want to speak with him."

"Two hermits? If they are related…"

"People can have the same last name without being related," Maddie pointed out.

"Fitz-Dankworthington?"

It was a stretch.

"Stranger things have happened." And in Louisiana? Stranger than strange things happened. A Rougarou had been a suspect in a case her brother Dan had investigated last year.

"If there is a connection…"

"When you find one, feel free to get back to me," Maddie said pleasantly.

"If I could just talk…"

"A lot of people want to talk to my client. I was hired to talk for him." Maddie made sure her tone was friendly, but final.

"He doesn't even have a photo on his book cover," the officer said.

"As I said, he is a very private individual." She sensed more questions coming and added, "and he hired me to protect that privacy for him. As his *lawyer*, I have a duty to honor his request."

"Thank you for your time." His voice was stiff. He cut the connection without waiting for her to respond.

Maddie leaned back, making the chair creak warningly, and rubbed her temples. It was too early in the morning for a headache. How deep was this guy willing to dig into her Fitz-D's life? It could get awkward.

On the upside, there was absolutely no connection between her hermit and theirs—if one didn't count the names. And she didn't.

MADDIE FIELDED calls from FitzD's editor, Helen, and a couple of reporters. They all got the same response. The reports of his death were premature.

Helen was harder to get rid of than the reporters. She really wanted to talk to him herself. But she always did. Her curiosity about Fitz-D grew with each book.

When Helen had negotiated the contact with Maddie, she'd been a lot less curious. Helen had been sure the book would do well, but no one ever knew how well any book would do. So agreeing to the privacy concerns hadn't been a problem.

When that book had unexpectedly hit several bestsellers lists and been a BookTok sensation, Helen had tried to find out more.

"My client is thrilled the book is doing so well, but he remains committed to preserving his privacy." Maddie knew her legalese, even if she hadn't much enjoyed deploying it in a minor capacity at her former firm.

Now Helen made another bid for more transparency.

"With this story, readers are going to want to know more," Helen pointed out.

"You know he designated me as his spokesperson, Helen. He just..." Maddie let the sentence trail off because she'd said it over and over again. "It's in his contract with me and with you."

"What is his problem?" Helen sounded irate.

Recognizing that thinking Fitz-D was dead had given her day a bad start, Maddie tried to be patient.

"He's just quirky, Helen. He barely speaks to me." Helen started to interrupt, and Maddie hurried into speech. "He trusts us to respect his wishes so he can write."

"Well, there is that. Is the next book coming along?"

"It is. I can probably get you some preliminary chapters..."

"I wouldn't have time to read them anyway." In a grudging tone, she added, "He always delivers and since he isn't dead..."

Maddie chuckled. "I can assure you he isn't dead."

On that upbeat note, Helen finally ended the call.

When her phone stayed silent for fifteen whole minutes, she began to hope that the two names were now in the process of being disconnected. Lucky for her, Gideon and Frank weren't in yet to hear her side of all those calls. They might actually get curious.

She sent out a couple of press releases herself and posted on her Fitz-D's social media accounts. It was a bit like watching a wave rolling ashore to see the news begin to spread.

She glanced at her watch? Only half an hour? It felt like she'd spent at least half the day working on this.

And thanks to Helen, she did have a few other author clients. Also, the office was due to open in a few. Time for Della to make her appearance.

With a grin, she pulled a small mirror out of the drawer without a lock and checked her appearance. She didn't look as frazzled as she felt. That was good.

She'd gradually eased out of her lawyer uniform, doing it slowly so her roommate wouldn't notice. Neither Gideon or Frank cared if she wore comfortable clothes. She couldn't see her tee shirt or jeans in the small mirror, but she'd seen them before she left the apartment.

Not exactly dressed to impress, but who was she going to impress here anyway?

The discreet bell on the outer door gave her a brief warning. Maddie put the mirror back in the drawer and closed it as she looked up, pasting on her Della Street smile.

No one coming through that door would be looking for her in either of her other guises.

The man's bulk filled the door frame and blocked the meager light from the hallway. It was, Madde decided, as she felt her heart speed up, fortunate that the light inside the office was adequate for the task of letting her see him.

He was very much worth seeing.

She wasn't sure how he managed to have both chiseled *and* rugged features, but she assigned some credit for that to the firm line of his mouth and his cool, blue eyes. Broad shoulders tapered down to lean hips in the classic romantic hero tradition.

His clothes were casual, but she had the sense that he'd worn a uniform at some point. He exuded crisp, almost lethal control like aftershave.

His gaze moved with deliberation around the small room. It didn't take him long, and what he thought about what he saw was absent from both eyes and face.

"This is *Baker Boys Investigations*?" he asked. His voice was smooth and deep with a slight husky undertone.

The door he held open with his body had the name clearly stenciled on the door, but she held her polite expression

"Yes, it is," she wanted half a beat, then asked, "how can we help you?"

He was a walk-in because there was no appointment on the schedule for either brother. Of course, they didn't always remember to update their schedules. But both usually managed to show up for appointments they'd made themselves.

His gaze moved to meet hers with what felt like more intent than the moment called for.

"You're M. Baker?"

Maddie wasn't sure whether to be offended or wary. She clearly wasn't a Baker Boy, but M. Baker was her literary lawyer handle and her desk was devoid of a name plate for a reason— and not just lack of space. On the other hand...she gave a slight nod, the Della Street expression giving way to wary.

If he was an author, this was not the way to approach her. She didn't use this address for her business address.

There was no chair to offer him as he stepped in and managed to close the door to the hall. His shoulders were wide enough to hide the door from her.

He towered over her, but she resisted the urge to rise and face him. Or to give into sudden claustrophobia. It had to be that and not because the guy was as hot as the sun.

She assumed what one of her professors had called, the position, as if she were in court. One foot slightly forward, her body angled into a position of polite attention.

"What can I do for you, Mr..."

"Quinn Ellery." His gaze narrowed, as if he were trying to figure her out.

Good luck with that, she thought. She had six brothers, seven sisters, and was the youngest of them, which meant they'd all had a hand in raising her. She couldn't even figure herself out after that.

"Is there somewhere we can sit down and talk?" he finally asked.

"That depends on what you want to talk about," Maddie said, matching him cool for cool.

He glanced at the closed doors. Maddie didn't tell him they were alone. She was the daughter of a cop and the sister of cops. She didn't do full disclosure.

"Look if you've written a book..." she began.

"No." Ellery hunched his shoulders, letting the first signs of emotion flicker across the quite pleasing planes of his face.

Before he could go on, the door handle rattled and then the door began to open. Ellery stepped quickly to one side, just missing getting the door in the back. Now Gideon filled the opening.

"Oh." He stopped, probably because there wasn't really room for him without some awkward maneuvering.

"Mr. Ellery, Gideon," Maddie said. They had a few cues they used to help him know what to expect from his clients, but not from hers.

"How can I help you?" Gideon said.

Ellery glanced at Maddie, but she declined to help him out.

"I'm here to see your...wife?"

She probably looked as horrified as Gideon. It was true that the Baker boys looked somewhat alike, and the Baker girls looked somewhat alike, but the guys and gals did not look that much like each other because they'd had different mothers.

"Maddie is my sister." Gideon gave her an annoyed look. She met his with one of hers.

"Do you think Frank would mind if we used his office for a few?" Maddie asked. Now that they weren't alone in the office, it would be better to get private before this guy asked her the wrong question in front of Gideon.

"He's not coming in until after lunch," Gideon said. "Sure, he won't mind."

Maddie rose, grabbing her laptop in the move, and indicated Frank's door, letting Ellery be the one to open it. He'd have to go first. It was the only way the flow of movement could happen.

She followed him in, looking back to see what Gideon thought, but typically, he was already closing the door to his office. She set the laptop down, sat down, and opened it. She looked up and saw Ellery's gaze on it. "I'm the receptionist."

"You're a receptionist and a lawyer?" His brows rose.

It didn't faze Maddie. "It's complicated."

He cautiously lowered himself into the other chair. He was correct to be concerned. It looked sleek but was flimsy. The chair creaked but held. He looked relieved.

"You don't look alike," Ellery said. "You and your brother."

"No, we don't," she agreed.

There was a brief silence while she looked at him looking at her.

"You're hard to track down," he said.

She might have thought it was funny that he was the fifth person to say that to her today, but this guy had tracked her *here*.

"Yes," she said. If he was trying to get her to start talking, he'd be disappointed. It was Lawyer 101 to never say more than was necessary and even then, don't say what's necessary if you can get away with it.

Ellery hesitated, but when it became clear she didn't plan to elucidate, he shifted in the uncomfortable chair and said, "I'm sure you've heard about Solice."

For a minute her mind blanked. Oh, *Solice*. The dead Fitz-D. She nodded.

"I was Sol's neighbor. I was the one who found him"

"I'm sorry." She didn't know what else to add to that. Had Sol been a good or difficult neighbor?

"You must have known how he was." The strong lips twitched a little.

"Actually, I didn't. Despite what the papers say, your Sol and my client are not the same person."

"I didn't think he could be," Ellery said.

Maddie bit back the question of why he was there then.

"The Sol I knew found it annoying to read the newspaper."

"Reading rates are down in the US," Maddie said. He was lucky this wasn't a legal visit. If she were charging him by the hour...

"The thing is, he was just a harmless old man who liked to be left alone." He paused.

Was she supposed to say something? She gave a slight nod.

"Why would someone bother to murder him?"

2

Finally, a reaction from the lady. She was a cool blonde, nice-looking, and he'd bet she had great legs. A pity she'd chosen to cover them in jeans, though the jeans did make her rear view pleasant. He'd been careful not to look too pointedly, of course. Not with her brother watching.

He found it hard to figure out what to say next. It was instinct that had brought him here. It had seemed obvious to find out if Sol was an author—even though the idea was ludicrous. And he'd been right. But that left him without a reason for the old boy to get murdered.

Or how to explain to her why he was there.

"His house," Quinn said slowly, his mind replaying the moment he'd found him. Sol had been a tidy hermit and not even especially irascible. He'd just wanted to be left alone. "Whoever killed him was looking for something."

He pulled himself back to the present and studied her. M. Baker. *Maddie.* Short for Madeline? M. Baker sounded important, contained, reserved. Maddie sounded like none of those things. And how she looked? Maybe a little of both.

"And you think," she hesitated as if reluctant to continue, "it had something to do with my author?"

She didn't sound incredulous, just skeptical.

"Well, your author," he decided he didn't have the energy to use the guy's full name, "writes books about unsolved mysteries, murders."

"My author writes fictional *re-imaginings* of unsolved mysteries. It's an intellectual, *fictional* exercise that his readers seem to like."

He didn't imagine the emphasis she put on fictional. He could concede that based on his two-day study of the guy's publication history, it was a stretch to think someone cared enough to kill over what were basically a reimagining of old murders.

"I noticed he's releasing a new book soon. There are mentions it's about the Calder murders."

"They happened twenty years ago," she pointed out.

"The real murderer was never found and could still be alive," he pointed back.

"But..."

"I know it's a stretch," he admitted. There was no way for anyone to know now how accurate her author had been in identifying the real killers in previous books. But from what he'd read, a lot of people thought the books were real. "But there's nothing I know of in Sol's life that could get him killed."

"There's nothing you *know*," she said. "How well did you know him?"

It was a fair question. Sol had been ex-military, which made his death even more unsettling, Quinn thought. A couple of kids had tried to prank him a few years back by pretending to be home invaders. They'd both ended up on the floor with his knees in their backs crying for mercy.

Granted, he'd aged since then, but—it just felt wrong. Off.

"Just for a moment, let's say Sol was killed because someone thought he was an author. Your guy could be in danger."

He didn't like that he'd said the words out loud, but to give her credit she didn't laugh at him.

"You've read the book," he said. "Is there anyone still alive who might not want this book released?"

"I'm not the only one who has read it, Mr. Ellery. His editor and others at the publisher have read it and review copies have gone out. If someone wanted to stop it, they needed to begin two years ago. There is another book in the pipeline and he's already working on a new book..."

His brows arched despite his determination to not.

She stopped. "There's no way anyone could know the content of that book."

"You're sure?"

She hesitated. "His editor has minimal information, and I've read some of it, but if I wanted to kill my client, I'd know where to find him."

He couldn't argue with that. "But there is information floating around the publisher's office?"

Quinn heard the outer doorbell sound and saw her glance down and frown. It was the most expression he'd seen on her face.

"What is it?" He was on his feet without conscious thought and yanked the door open.

The masked punk couldn't show surprise, but he reared back into the edge of the still open door. It must have hurt because he yelped, spun around, and took off with a definite hitch to his gait. Quinn briefly considered going after him.

"He's gone?" M. Baker spoke behind him. "No point going after him. The door wasn't locked, and he didn't have time to do anything."

Yeah, she was a lawyer.

He glanced at the other door.

With some reluctance, she said, "He went out."

"I didn't hear the bell."

"His room has another exit."

Quinn noted that her posture had gotten more defensive.

"That punk couldn't have known I was coming here," he said. "He must have thought you were alone."

"I would have locked the door, and we do have a surveillance camera, but he couldn't have known that," she admitted to with what looked like reluctance.

Quinn glanced around, but couldn't spot the camera. "I'm glad to hear it."

He had the feeling that she might be thinking as hard as he was about what had just happened. His gaze slid down to the laptop now held against her chest. "Do you think he could have been after that? Do you have samples of the new book on there?"

She eased around him until her desk was between them. "That would be my client's business, Mr Ellery."

Her tone said he was really reaching now, which he was.

"But what if he was after that? What's the story about this time?" He knew, even as he asked the question, she wasn't going to answer it. Why should she? She didn't know him. And she did know her business. Despite working here ostensibly as a receptionist, he had a feeling she knew her stuff.

"I don't like leaving you alone here," he said, into her silence. When she didn't speak, he added, "We could go get lunch?"

"It's ten o'clock."

But she looked amused.

"Brunch then." This was New Orleans. They'd have brunch somewhere. It surprised him how much he wanted her to accept the offer.

She studied him and then, to his surprise, nodded.

"Okay, but we walk somewhere."

"That's fine."

"Okay then, Mr. Ellery." She sat at her desk and after a few seconds removed a purse and a laptop bag. She stowed her laptop and slung that bag and her purse over her shoulder.

"Call me Quinn, Ms. Baker," he suggested.

"Quinn." Did she hesitate? "Call me Maddie."

"Maddie," he repeated. He liked saying it. He took a careful breath, taking in the warm, sweet smell of her. "Shall we go?"

MADDIE LOCKED the office and then walked next to Quinn down the hallway to the stairs. At the door to the street, she came face-to-face with Gideon.

"Maddie?" Gideon said, his gaze moving from her face to Quinn's and then back to hers.

"Gideon," Maddie said, stepping to one side. Maddie recognized the look. Her brothers could be impressively clueless, but when they got curious, look out. But there was also the family rule of not airing family business in front of strangers.

Gideon stepped back, but Maddie could tell he'd just put a pause on curiosity. She donned her sunglasses and gave him a sweet smile. That annoyed him, which had been her purpose. *For what did she live but to make sport for her brothers and laugh at them in her turn?* She kept her grin internal but had a feeling that Jane Austen would approve of the rewrite.

Out of the corner of her eye, she saw an SUV with black tinted windows cruise slowly past. She turned to follow it, automatically noting the license plate. It was a thing in her family. Growing up, she'd never known when Zach would ask if they knew the license plate of a car that had just passed out of sight.

The SUV sped up and turned the corner out of sight.

"You get the plate number?" Gideon asked.

With a sigh, Maddie told him.

"That's what I got," Gideon said, pulling out his phone and noting it down.

Now it was Quinn's turn to look curious.

"My dad is a retired cop. It's a thing to improve our memory." Quinn's brows arched just slightly in disbelief. "Yeah, I didn't believe that either."

Zach had tried to give them all good situational awareness. Just because her dad was a bit paranoid didn't mean they hadn't needed it from time to time. Maddie also had a concealed carry permit. It was another reason she'd resigned from her law firm. She didn't like being in gun-free zones.

Maddie glanced at Quinn as they began to stroll down the narrow street. He definitely had situational awareness, too. Since he had taken the forward view, she made sure to keep an eye on the rear. Her sunglasses were a gift from her sister-in-law—who seemed to have access to some pretty cool tech. It had taken some getting used to, having the little frame in the glasses showing her what was happening behind her.

"This okay?" Quinn asked, indicating a small cafe. Maddie indicated assent and he held the door open for her, once again scanning the street before he followed her in.

It was dim inside and the rich scent of a multiplicity of spices hung deliciously in the air. No other city smelled quite like New Orleans. And if one excluded the touristy eating places, it was almost impossible to get bad food in even the smallest cafe.

Quinn chose a small table in the rear and held out the chair that put her back to the door. She sat, reluctantly removing her sunglasses and stowing them in her bag. She tucked both of her bags securely between her legs, and then rested her elbows on the table, and turned to study the menu affixed to the wall.

She wasn't actually hungry, but one didn't have to be hungry to have a beignet. Quinn followed her lead, though he added a cup of coffee. When they were alone again, she decided he wasn't sure where to start. She couldn't help him because she didn't know what he'd hoped to find out by approaching her. This couldn't just be about a book. There was the murder, she knew, but it was a huge stretch to think it was connected to Fitz-D, wasn't it?

Maddie poked at her beignet with a finger, then looked up. "Why are you really here?"

His stoic mien softened into a grin that made her heart stutter. "I'm not sure," he admitted. He leaned back, heaving an audible sigh and shoved a hand through his hair.

Maddie looked away. It wasn't very proper to envy that hand. She made herself meet his gaze and liked that he met it squarely but also kept checking their surroundings. He felt safe, like her brothers, not that she'd admit that to them—but also in an unbrotherly way. So many times she'd meet nice looking guys who did and said the right things but just gave off the wrong vibe. So far, her instincts had never let her down.

If she took a mental step back and considered him as a guy, a dude who'd come all this way for his dead neighbor...he was following his instincts, she realized. He didn't like it, but he was doing it. She liked that. She'd grown up surrounded by guys and gals who did the right thing, even when it was uncomfortable and occasionally inexplicable..

She looked down at her plate and rolled up a crumb of powdered sugar, then pressed it flat.

"Your gut is telling you something, isn't it?" Then she looked up again.

He gave a nod. "It is."

"You've been in the military." It was not a question, but if he wanted to answer her, that would be great. It would help her place him and his gut instinct.

"SEAL. I left...a couple of years ago."

She could fill in that blank. Her brother Frank had been pushed out of the FBI, too.

"I have six brothers," she said and watched him flinch. He didn't pale like some of her dates had, but he had been a SEAL. And he wasn't a date.

"Okay."

"Cops, former FBI, Coast Guard, SWAT. I get instincts. I'm surrounded by instincts. And if you tell them this, I'll deny it, but I trust their instincts."

He studied her carefully, his gaze definitely thoughtful. She liked the look of it on his face. Okay, she hadn't yet seen a look on his face she didn't like, but they'd known each what, half an hour? There was still time.

"Are you saying you trust *my* instincts?"

"I'm saying, I respect them, and I might...consider them as valid."

"You sound like a lawyer." He grinned again.

Her toes might have curled. She sternly admonished them. This was not the time to let emotion cloud her judgment. But the weird thing was, she didn't feel clouded. She felt sharply aware and on her game.

She hesitated, and then decided to do it. If there was some connection...

"I'm going to tell you something that my six brothers and six sisters—"

"You have *six* sisters, too?"

She waved a hand as if to brush the question away. "Zach is an over achiever."

He blinked, swallowed and nodded. She decided to give him a minute to collect himself. Even SEAL training couldn't train someone for the reality of thirteen kids.

"I'm sorry," he said. "Please go on."

"No one knows this. *No one.*"

He leaned forward, gaze intent.

"S.C Fitz-Dankworthington *is* the pseudonym." Suddenly it felt as if her feet were teetering on the edge of a cliff. If she said the words out loud, everything would change.

"Your client," he stopped and frowned. "What about client privilege?"

She just looked at him and waited. If he figured it out on his own, she'd officially be impressed. And if he didn't? She'd still be impressed, just not as much.

His eyes widened. "*You're...*"

Maybe it was because of the shock that he couldn't say the name. Maybe it was because it was a painful name to say. But he'd got it. She saw it in his eyes.

"Yes," she said. "I'm my client."

As the shock began to wear off, Quinn began to wonder why she'd told *him*.

Instincts. She'd started with instincts. His and... hers? It was one of a long list of questions multiplying inside his head.

No one else knows this.

She met his gaze with a calm that impressed him. She might even be a little amused. Okay, if he were on the other side of the situation, he'd be more than a little amused.

"The name, why?" It was a place to begin, he decided.

"I happened across it, and I thought it was funny," she said. "And when I did it, I was just putting a book out there for fun. I was yet another lawyer who'd written a book. I never expected..." She stopped and rubbed her nose, then gave him a wry grin.

Quinn felt the shock of it all the way to his toes. He hoped his eyes didn't cross. He pulled his gaze off her face and did a sweep of the room and felt his spine stiffen as a woman came in. She didn't appear dangerous but there was something in the way she moved and in the way her gaze found them then jerked away.

Those instincts kicking in again.

The woman took the seat with her back to Maddie. It was true there weren't a lot of tables, but people usually tried for separation when it was available to them. Well, he did.

Her chair was angled just enough that he saw her shift in the seat. She put her hands in her lap, then lifted them to rest on the table. Her fingers closed and then opened.

He took in these details as Maddie went on. It took him a moment to realize she'd changed the subject.

"And then I told him, no way. Wasn't going to happen."

He flicked a glance at her, caught the intent look in her eyes. What had she sensed that made her change the subject? At least she hadn't asked him about the Saints.

"And what did he say?" Quinn asked, his gaze resuming its sweep as he played along.

"Oh, he blustered for a bit, but what was he going to do?" She shifted a little more, edging her chair so that it wasn't quite behind the woman's.

"Nice win," he said. Someone walked past the restaurant door, then reappeared heading the other direction. The next time he—Quinn was sure it was a he—he'd pulled something down over his face.

The intruder yanked the door open and surged inside, waving a handgun around.

"No one move!"

Quinn took time to give Maddie a look he hoped was reassuring and a warning not to move.

The kid headed straight for them. Quinn thought Maddie might have moved a little, but he didn't, he couldn't take his eyes off the intruder. Didn't take a SEAL to know this guy didn't have the moves to take on a SEAL.

The woman behind Maddie half-turned and the intruder didn't say anything to her, just stayed focused on Quinn.

When he was close enough, Quinn caught his wrist, twisting it and turning the weapon up, then moving fluidly in to take him down to the floor, his knee pressed into the perp's back, the arm twisted painfully back.

The handgun dropped to the floor with a thud.

He heard Maddie say, "I wouldn't if I were you."

He looked over and saw Maddie holding a weapon with impressive resolve against the woman's temple. The woman, he noted, had a hand on the handle of Maddie's laptop bag.

"Put your hands under your knees."

Quinn twitched at the tone of her voice and almost put his hands under his knees. He didn't, of course.

He glanced at Maddie. They made a pretty good team.

"I've called 911," their waiter said.

Quinn wondered why this statement made her grimace.

To Maddie's relief it was a patrol unit that showed up. It was not a long-lasting relief, however. She'd just finished giving her statement when she saw her brother, Alex, pushing his way through the inevitable crowd outside. Was it an official "baking" of the scene if it were just the two of them? This was her first time in this situation.

"I'm sorry," she said in aside to Quinn.

"For what?" he asked.

"I told you I have six brothers. That's the oldest of them." She nodded her chin toward the door swinging inward yet again. Alex's shoulders filled the doorway and then some. He'd always cast a big shadow. One of the uniforms must have tipped him off because his gaze scanned the room and found her immediately.

She lifted her hand in a sort of wave. Did it look as resigned as it felt?

The interior was tight but somehow Alex managed to make a path to her. Beside her Quinn rose to his feet and she followed suit. Alex still loomed over her, but his attention was fixed on Quinn.

"Alex, this is Quinn Ellery. Quinn, this is my brother, Alex." She watched them size each other up. Quinn was younger than Alex, but the SEAL thing evened things out a lot.

They shook hands. She couldn't tell if they did the male dominance thing. Their grip ended after what seemed to her to be a reasonable time. She released a tiny sigh. She'd been holding her breath. Wow.

Her brother's gaze swung her way and she knew he waited for her to rush into speech about who Quinn was and what they were thinking to get almost mugged in broad daylight in a coffee shop. But she wasn't a kid anymore. She repeated that to herself a couple more times because Alex was totally bringing the big brother vibe down on her.

The difference this time, she'd been through law school and been a sad and lowly intern in a law firm with a boss who could have given Cruella de Vil a run for her money, and now she was basically her own boss.

It was Alex who finally broke the silence.

"I didn't expect to see you down this way this time of day, Maddie."

It *was* a long way from where she had worked. It might have been a mistake not to tell her family she'd quit her job. It wasn't like it was a desperate or even dirty secret. It was just that they were always so much up in her grill about everything. And they'd want to know how she paid her bills and she wasn't ready to tell them that yet.

All of her siblings had a beef about what it had been like to be this age or that age in a line up of thirteen. Alex claimed he'd had the hardest lot because he'd raised them all and there'd been no one to raise him. And the others because they'd been raised by siblings—or wolves her sisters liked to claim. Everyone'd had a lot of sibling oversight, but no one'd had more than Maddie. Hadn't been taken seriously growing up? Try being her, she thought and felt her mouth curving into a mutinous line she'd tried to get over.

She straightened her lips and said, "Can we get out of here? We've both given our statements."

Alex glanced around, shot a question at one of the uniforms and got permission.

He cleared a path for them just by sheer presence, reality being more important than "ladies first."

He didn't ask them to follow him, but they did. Maddie gave Quinn a wry, apologetic glance and he grinned—a grin that was gone before Alex could note it when he glanced back at them.

No question Alex had alpha instincts. He'd probably sensed the exchange of glances. She gave Quinn props for his quick reactions. Not that she was surprised. Even as she'd been engaged in stopping that woman from stealing her laptop, she'd been able to note the quick and easy way Quinn had taken the guy down. He hadn't even broken a sweat.

It had been better than an action movie scene to watch him.

"Nice job stopping that woman," Quinn said, not bothering to lower his voice for Alex. "Was she after your laptop?"

"Yeah, stupid move. I have it locked down and backed up." With encryption she could have added, thanks to the same sister-in-law who'd given her the cool sunglasses. "All they'd have got was an expensive brick." And she'd have had to figure out how to add the expense of a new laptop into her already tight budget.

She noted the way Alex's shoulders stiffened, but he didn't speak. He wouldn't. Not in front of Quinn. Right now, he'd be wondering if he wanted to get rid of Quinn so he could grill Maddie, or if he wanted to get Quinn alone for the grilling first.

Alex stopped at the entrance to the office. Well, at least she'd be back where this party started.

Then Alex hesitated. "Do you think Gideon or Frank are here?"

Last she knew he was there, but he could have left again. If Gideon hadn't left, he'd give the show away by not being surprised to see her. Oh well, it had been good while it lasted.

"I have a key," she said coolly and took the lead, acutely aware of two very masculine sets of footsteps hitting the wooden floors behind her, not to mention the big brother gaze slamming her between the shoulder blades like the hammer of the gods.

She needed time to think, but she had a feeling she wasn't going to get it. It wasn't like she didn't know that her chickens were coming home to roost. But they wouldn't land until they were alone. Her brothers took a lot on themselves, but Alex wouldn't dress her down in front of Quinn. She hoped. She used the time to assemble her lawyer mode, the full-on version that no one in her family had seen yet.

QUINN KNEW BETTER than to grin, but inside he chuckled. He carefully didn't look at big brother as they took the stairs up. Even if Maddie hadn't told him, Quinn would have known that Alex was the eldest. First children—especially the guys—recognized each other. He wondered where Maddie was in the thirteen-child pecking order.

That was a little harder to tell. *Zach was an over achiever.* That had to be an understatement.

He figured he had two issues to figure out before they were back at the office.

Was he wasting his time here?

Would Maddie tell her brother anything? *No one knows.* And if she did tell him, how much did he tell her big brother?

Was that just two issues? Or three?

It was annoying that their talk had been interrupted just as it was starting to get really interesting. But if or when he learned more, would it matter? Did she actually know something?

They reached the office before he could come to any conclusion. The door wasn't locked. Inside the tight space of the reception area, Maddie moved back behind her desk and regarded her brother with a composure Quinn found hard to quantify.

It wasn't defiance, but it wasn't compliance either. He crossed his arms over his chest, leaned against the wall and waited.

The silence was just starting to get awkward when Gideon opened his door and stopped, looking at Alex and then Maddie.

"Problem?"

Maddie gave a half shrug that could have meant anything.

"Maddie was almost mugged," Alex said, "just down the street."

Gideon's expression turned to concern. "You all right?"

"I'm fine. Quinn took the perp down like a Navy SEAL."

Gideon looked impressed. "Thanks."

"You're welcome," Quinn said, giving a short, sharp nod.

Gideon turned back to Maddie. "I added an appointment to the schedule."

He said it like he thought he ought to get a medal for it.

"Good job," Maddie said.

Alex made a movement, but there wasn't anywhere in the place to take it. Maddie had said no one knew about the books, but this felt like Alex didn't know she worked there. Would he admit it?

"I'd better get going," Alex said abruptly. "Glad you're okay, Maddie." He shot Quinn a look that was also hard to parse. "Thanks for looking out for her."

"You're welcome," Quinn said again. He thought about adding that Maddie probably could have handled both of them but then decided against it. Big brother was leaving. Time to let him.

"I'll see you later, Maddie," Alex said before easing out the door and shutting it with careful emphasis.

"Was that a threat?" Gideon asked, one brow rising.

"Probably," Maddie said. Gideon's other brow rose. "He might not have heard that I quit my job and have been helping out here."

"Oh."

Quinn had wondered what a pregnant silence would be like. Now he knew.

"Okay then." Gideon gestured at the office behind him. "I'll just get back to work."

The door closed before either he or Maddie could respond. Quinn repressed a grin

Maddie didn't try. "It's okay. You can laugh if you want to."

Quinn let out a chuckle and liked the way her eyes brightened as the air of reserve fell away.

She stepped away from her desk and rapped lightly on the door of the office they'd used before. When there was no answer, she opened it.

"Shall we try again or are you over the baking?"

"Baking?" His brows shot up now..

"It's a thing that happens to a scene when more than two of us are gathered in one place," she explained.

Quinn did remember her listing off what law enforcement related things her family did.

"Oh." He hesitated. "I still have questions. I'm not sure if they are...relevant." Or if he even had a right to know the answers.

"It's your call. You know my deepest, darkest secret. There's not a lot more to find out."

So why did he have the feeling she wanted him to stay?

"I'll admit I'm curious," he admitted. And if he walked away now? He might lose more than answers to questions he didn't have a right to ask. What more? He didn't know that either.

"If you cross the line, I'll shut you down."

She slid into the room and this time she didn't open her laptop, just stowed it and her purse out of sight behind the desk.

He had a strange sense of *deja vu* mixed with anticipation as he once more carefully lowered himself into a chair that didn't look strong enough to support a toddler.

4

Maddie pulled out a drawer that Frank had filled with a small, portable refrigerator and extracted two expensive bottles of water. He wouldn't like it, but he'd have to get over it. She couldn't afford to replace it.

She handed one to Quinn and opened the other, lifting it to let the cool stream of water slide down her throat. She lowered her chin to find Quinn's gaze on her, a curious little flame in the backs of his eyes.

Color rose in her cheeks, and she looked down, setting the bottle on the desktop but keeping her hands clasped around it. The careful lawyer persona she'd built up to deal with Alex had left and she felt weirdly vulnerable, despite the handgun she'd returned to its holster.

Perhaps Quinn realized she didn't know how to restart the conversation.

"So you're Fitz-Dankworthington."

It didn't seem quite as funny now that his neighbor—friend—had been murdered. Was there a connection? It felt like such a stretch and yet...

Quinn was here.

And against all logic, she sensed there might be a connection. But what? Her published books were out there. Could someone have found out what she was working on now?

Her editor had the barest information on four possible cases she'd thought about fictionalizing. It had been five, but that book was now in the pipeline. Two had been set aside for now. And the third was her current work in progress. If—and that was a huge if—the murder and the mugging were linked to one of those cases...

"I'm afraid so."

"You said no one knows, but surely your publisher..."

Maddie shook her head. "I meant it when I said you were the only other person."

Was it stupid to admit that? In a movie it would be stupid to admit he was the only one who knew but this wasn't a movie. And if he was here to stop her, he was going about it in a really weird way. Saving her from a mugging. Meeting her brothers.

"Do you think that's why someone tried to steal your laptop? To find out?"

If it had just been one weird thing today, Maddie would have scoffed. It was hard to scoff when someone had invaded the office and then tried to mug them. It was New Orleans, but that did still seem to defy the odds

"You are known to be...your agent." He gave a rueful smile as if he knew the sentence was funny.

"I did need a forward face for the books," Maddie admitted. "And I picked up some other clients."

"Did you recommend yourself?"

Maddie laughed. "I didn't stoop quite that low. My editor sent them to me."

He was quiet for a minute. "You said you published your first book yourself?"

"I did. When Helen reached out to me, at first I wasn't interested." Self-publishing was lovely. Being her own boss was even better than lovely.

"Reached out to you?" Quinn raised a brow at her and Maddie grinned.

"I did a good job of obscuring my trail, but I did need a front facing person, even as a nobody author. So, I made me that person. So yeah, she talked to me." Maddie leaned back, recalling the negotiations, the clauses she'd required to be struck from the contract. She'd done a lot of research as they went along.

And it had dawned on her that this might be her ticket out of the firm.

Helen's belief that the books could do well had been realized. Maddie had given up some income to get into bookstores and some publishing autonomy, but it had paid off. And she still had plans to pursue some self-published projects. One thing she'd learned from the indie publishing community: don't put all your eggs in one basket.

She wasn't making quite enough yet to have a comfortable financial cushion, but the potential was there. And she was careful with the money she was making.

Publishing was a crazy business, filled with a lot of uncertainty and risk. Did she like not having a steady paycheck? Not really. But the strings attached to steady were cloying and clinging and she'd ended every workday feeling like she'd been in the boxing ring, not an office. She'd cut the strings and had no regrets.

It was funny that her books—which took old, unsolved crimes and "solved" them—had taken off as well as they had. The last had hit the *New York Times* and the *USA Today* best seller lists.

And someone had died. She sighed.

"How do you do it?" Quinn asked.

She pulled herself back into the present. "Do what?"

"Solve the crimes?"

"I don't actually solve anything." She leaned back. It was nice to actually talk to someone about it. She'd need to be careful, though. "The first one, I watched a show about it and got the idea of how and who."

That had been kind of fun. No one was alive to say she was right or wrong, but readers were like, yeah, that makes total sense.

It was trickier with the books that followed. Not all the unsolved crimes that caught her attention were far enough in the past for everyone involved to be dead.

She'd picked her way with care. And the one she was working on now? It was definitely higher risk—not of death but of a defamation suit.

If she was right? He'd totally gotten away with it. She was basically tiptoeing through a minefield.

"Your readers think you're right," Quinn pointed out.

"Well, I write *to* make them think I'm right."

"Like a lawyer." He grinned.

"Exactly like a lawyer." She grinned back. "It's—not easy exactly—but it's possible to make your case more clearly without pesky defense lawyers or judges mucking things up."

Quinn laughed outright at that. He sobered. "You have an interesting mind." He hesitated, "I read your last one before I came here. I'd have sworn it was written like a man would."

"Six brothers," Maddie said. "Zach, my dad, is a retired cop, and yeah, a lot of law enforcing in my life."

"But six sisters," Quinn said.

"We were swimming up stream all the time," Maddie said. "They are great, and I love them, but my sister claims we were raised by wolves and I'm not sure she's wrong."

Maddie smiled to herself, but she watched Quinn from

under her lashes. He knew more than anyone right now. Was it enough? Or would he ask that last question?

He didn't leave her doubt.

"I know I don't have the right to ask this, but what is your next book about?"

And there it was.

It was none of his business. But what if it had cost that man his life? As Miss Marple liked to point out, murder might sleep, but it doesn't go away.

It felt so weird to consider that she might know who the killer was and have no way to prove it. Unless he killed again.

Or he had already killed again.

QUINN WAITED, watching her consider. He couldn't tell which way she'd go. So he decided to just ask.

"Is it the Ashbourne case?"

She studied him thoughtfully, still not giving much away. "It is on the list of cases I've been," she hesitated, "considering working on."

He felt a stab of something. Was it worry? Disappointment? A little of both maybe. He'd hoped...

"That kind of widens the field," he said.

"I had thought of that, *if* this is about my books." She sounded doubtful, but she hadn't kicked him out yet.

"For the cases on your list, do you already know who you think did it?"

She was quiet for several seconds. "A case doesn't make it on my list unless I have an idea."

"How do you decide which one to work on?"

It wasn't exactly a yes or no.

"Well, obviously it needs to be a compelling story or have the potential to be compelling, but..."

When she didn't continue, he prompted, "but?"

"I'm a lawyer. I don't want to get sued. I have to tread carefully if anyone is still alive."

"How long is your list?"

"I'm down to three," she admitted. "But there's no guarantee that I'll pick one of them next. That was just a list I made up for Helen a few years back."

"But still, three possible cases." He felt like he was feeling his way in the dark.

"Why did you think I might be working on the Ashbourne case?"

"It's unsolved. Lots of drama," he hedged.

She studied him for what felt like an excruciatingly long time.

"There are a lot of unsolved cases out there like that," she said, finally. "If you got...curious...who's to say someone else didn't get equally curious. Again, if what happened today is about the books."

She sensed it was more than curiosity, but she hadn't called him out on it yet.

He'd come here hoping for an answer and he'd found more questions. And something he wasn't ready to face just yet. Despite this, or maybe because of it—he was a guy, so he didn't know—the silence wasn't uncomfortable. She was working something out in her head. He'd bet she was a good lawyer.

"You're not in regular practice?" he asked before he thought about it.

Her gaze focused and her brows rose. "I was in a firm. I didn't much like it."

"You did regular law?" He pressed.

"I wasn't a prosecutor or a defense attorney if that's what

you're asking. I wanted to forge a different path." The slight grimace at the end of this made Quinn smile.

"Bit of a head wind going against the family?"

"A bit. And my family has a love/hate relationship with lawyers. They love them when they need them and when they get in their way..."

"I can imagine." He could. "You're the...youngest?"

"Is it that obvious?"

"No, though Alex was. I'm an oldest, too," he admitted.

"They say we recognize our own kind." She chuckled, then fell silent. "What...where...why are we here?"

All she needed to add was when and how. At least she'd said "we."

"I'm feeling my way," he said.

"I get that."

He needed to just say it, get it out there. "I have personal reasons for being interested in the Ashbourne case. Family reasons."

"It's been a while since I did a deep dive into that case, but I don't remember the name Ellery being associated with it," Maddie said, speaking slowly, but not upset that he could see.

"It wouldn't be. This was on the female side, my mom's people." He hesitated. "You said you could see or guess who did it."

"And you want a name? What if I'm wrong?"

"What if you're not?" He didn't wait for her to speak again, just went on, "I know it's not proof. I get that. I'd just like to know." And it might be enough for his grandmother. Maybe. "What if that person killed Sol? Hired someone to steal your laptop?"

He knew he was stretching, but she didn't call him on it.

"Stealing my laptop wouldn't be enough to stop—"

"They wouldn't know that. You're the literary attorney. They think the author is someone else."

She sat back, took another drink from the sweating bottle of water, which made his thoughts flicker in the wrong direction. He pulled them back. She set the bottle down and carefully twisted the lid back on again.

"Let's just assume for a minute that everything you say is true. That someone is worried enough about what I'll write to do..." she waved a hand as if she couldn't bring herself to say it out loud, "what do you suggest I do about it?"

It was a good question, and he didn't have a good answer.

MADDIE WASN'T SURPRISED that Quinn couldn't answer her question. She felt stuck. Weirdly stuck because she didn't want to leave this room. Only she needed to leave this room.

She rose abruptly. "I need to visit the ladies'."

Quinn scrambled up and opened the door for her. He followed her out that door and then the other door into the hall. He followed her all the way to the ladies' room. She turned to face him before he could open that door for her.

"I'd like to do this by myself."

His lips twitched. She held back the urge to touch his firm mouth, trace it with the tip of a finger. She was losing the plot. For an author, that was a serious crime.

"I'll wait right here," he said.

She stared up at him, about to protest.

"What is a place that we all have to use at some point during the day?" He arched a brow. "If I wanted to to...talk...to you by myself without someone knowing, this is where I'd choose."

"The women's bathroom?"

He grinned and shrugged.

She bit back a grin and gave a half nod of agreement. She couldn't argue with that point. The call of nature was universal.

Inside, she closed the stall door, wincing at the creak. The walls were painfully thin and it took willpower to do her business. The squeak of her door was echoed by the stall at the end of the short row.

Maddie looked around as a woman emerged. A woman holding a handgun. She didn't even try to hide her sigh.

"Really?"

The woman might have been taken aback.

Without waiting to find out, Maddie turned to the sink and soaped her hands.

"We're leaving..." the woman hissed.

"I'm going to wash my hands." She met the woman's gaze in the mirror and began to count out loud to thirty. She saw the woman's mouth open to object, but it snapped closed.

Had she heard her and Quinn talking? It was possible, even likely. And yet here she was. If she knew Quinn was waiting outside...

"You're going to pretend everything is just fine. I don't want to hurt the boyfriend." Her voice was low and attempted threatening.

"Fine."

"Keep your voice down!" The woman clamped her lips together, then indicated the door. "You, first."

The woman stepped to the side of the door, pressing her back against the wall. Maddie reached out and pulled the door open, essentially hiding the woman, but also...

Quinn smashed the door into the woman.

The grunt was satisfying.

He was in the bathroom before the grunt finished. Maddie missed what happened next, because the door swung closed between them. She cocked her head to the side, but all she heard was a small moan.

She should probably call the cops. She didn't want to. Twice in a day was just embarrassing. And it would put her back on Alex's radar.

She cleared the doorway as the door opened again and Quinn stepped out.

He was alone.

Maddie tried to look past him, but the guy was built like a rock wall. So, she arched a brow at him instead.

"I happened to have some plastic restraints on me. I don't know about you, but calling 911 isn't what I'd advise—at least until we're clear."

"It's like you read my mind," Maddie said.

Quinn cupped her elbow, turning her back toward the office. "Let's get your stuff. Do you need to tell your brother something?"

Maddie looked at her watch. It was just coming onto noon. Longest. Day. Ever.

When she'd gathered up her things, Quinn didn't move.

"Is there another way out?"

"There is, but..." Did she really think someone was watching this building that closely?

Quinn studied her. "I wish you had a hat or something."

She glanced at Gideon's door. She did not want to bring him into the problem, at least not yet. But...she crossed and tapped lightly on the door. No answer. She eased the door open. He wasn't there.

"Gideon keeps a change of clothes in here. There might be something I can use," she said.

Quinn squeezed in after her and she crouched down and pulled open the drawer of his office "closet."

Even as she sorted through the clothes, a part of her was

wondering what the heck? Was she really about to go off with a man she'd met a couple of hours ago? A man who could have staged everything that had happened? A man, she shot him a look out of the corner of her eye—the best looking, most competent man she'd met lately who wasn't related to her.

"Someone is suddenly pushing hard," Quinn observed. She noted he had the door just cracked and was watching the little foyer.

She pulled out a tee shirt and pulled it over her head. It landed around her knees. A gimme cap was under it. She pulled it on and tucked her hair up in it. She had put on her sunglasses. They weren't outwardly distinctive. She regarded her handbag and laptop case a bit wryly.

They weren't particularly distinctive, but if someone had been watching.

"Frank," she said. "He'll have something, I'll bet."

Quinn didn't ask what she meant, just occupied the foyer while she found Frank's reusable shopping bags. One hid her purse, the other her laptop bag.

Quinn held out his hands for the bags.

"Don't you need to keep your hands free?"

"We'll each take one," he said.

Maddie kept her laptop, and he didn't object. She noticed that he used a clearing technique to check the hall. It wasn't hard to recognize based on her law enforcement intense family. But Quinn did bring some gravitas to the exercise.

"Clear," he said, then gave her a wry grin. "Old habits."

"Not a problem." At the doorway, she might have hesitated for a fraction of a moment. Was she really committing her safety to this man purely on instinct? She looked down, surprised to find her feet doing exactly that.

5

Their egress from the building had gone smoothly and without incident. There had been a gut-tightening five minutes while he retrieved his truck, leaving Maddie tucked into a shadowed doorway. He'd circled the block to see if he'd attracted attention, before returning to fetch her.

The relief he felt when she clambered into the cab was not comfortable and was also out of proportion to the situation.

He eased the truck through traffic, trying to keep an eye on their six. As far as he could tell they hadn't picked up a tail

"So now what?" Maddie asked. "If they found the office, they probably know where I live."

He heard the distaste in her voice.

"We need to stop, regroup, and figure this out," he said. He hadn't bothered to get a room. His plan had been to drive back tonight.

"Yeah."

He glanced over and caught her frowning, her fingers moving as if she were counting something.

"I have a couple of options that might work."

It was her city.

"My sister-in-law runs a catering service out of her house." She glanced at him. "It's a big house and there is a place in the back you could park."

Parking was always an issue in New Orleans.

"Downside?" He could tell there was one.

"Well, Alex, his wife and baby live there, too, with Sarah. And she's married to Cal who is SWAT. I don't like the idea of bringing possible danger there."

When she didn't speak right away, Quinn prompted, "Other options?" She had said she had a lot of siblings.

"There's Zach, my dad," she added.

Quinn felt his throat tighten. Dad. Parent. Father. Wouldn't be his first choice.

"Or if you didn't mind a bit of a drive, my other sister-in-law, Gemma, is part owner of a boat. I believe it's still in dock. I could call her and find out. And there are various other apartments. Gideon's wife is cool. Frank lives alone."

"We might need to avoid anyone obviously Baker," Quinn suggested. "The boat sounds...interesting." And it might be unexpected. "We just need to drop out of sight long enough to figure out what's going on." He said it optimistically, though was far from it. He'd come here hoping to discuss one case, one solution, not three or more. Because they didn't know if Maddie was even interested in the case that was giving her problems at the moment.

"I'll make the call," Maddie said. "Dan used to be Coast Guard, but he and Gemma are NCIS now."

Quinn blinked a little.

"Turn here," Maddie directed. "We'll need to cross the bridge." And then, "Gemma, I have a favor to ask, a keep-it-on-the-down-low favor."

He could tell from Maddie's side of the conversation that Gemma had no problem with the down-low part. And he also learned something new about this woman he'd just met.

She knew how to talk without giving much away. At one point, Maddie had given him a side-long look, possibly from a question from Gemma, because she'd grinned and said, "Something like that."

When she ended the call, Quinn said, "She sounds interesting."

Maddie's grin might have been wicked. "You have no idea."

THEY STOPPED before they left the city to buy essential toiletries and a change of clothes and then Maddie directed Quinn to the twisting, winding road that took them Gulf bound toward the bayou where the *Real Escape* was moored. Gemma's partner, Little Abner was aboard and she'd let him know they were coming.

"He'll make raisin bread with bologna for you, but he doesn't actually want you to eat it," Gemma said.

"That is good to know," Maddie had told her before ringing off. She looked at Quinn. "We don't have to eat the raisin bread and bologna sandwiches if Little Abner offers them."

"You're right," Quinn said. "That is good to know." A pause. "Little Abner?"

"He's the co-owner of the *Reel Escape*," Maddie said. She didn't know a lot about him, and she hoped she'd be glad to know more.

Maddie shifted restlessly in her seat, not because it was uncomfortable, but because her brain was bouncing all over the place wondering, who, what, when, how, why. Normally she'd deal with this state by writing. The bumpy winding road didn't lend itself to typing.

As if he sensed her disquiet, Quinn said, "We could talk about the cases."

She angled in the seatbelt so she could study him. Like her, he'd donned sunglasses, and they needed them as the afternoon sun stabbed almost perfectly into the truck's cab. He'd taken off his jacket at some point before he'd picked her up. His tee shirt revealed strong, muscular arms and the hands on the steering wheel were relaxed and confident.

She felt both safe and a bit tingly at the sight of him. And liking. She felt liking.

She wanted to ask him what it was like to be a SEAL, but he was right. They should talk about the possible cases. She couldn't just disappear from her life for too long. Just because her dad had thirteen kids to keep track of, didn't mean he wouldn't notice if one of them dropped off the radar for too long. Zach had instincts, too, well-honed ones.

"The Ashbourne case?" She'd have trouble pulling on the details off the top of her head. She'd rather wait until they were stopped, and she could look at her notes.

He hesitated, then shook his head. "What are you working on right now?"

"It's the Calder case," Maddie admitted. "It's about two-thirds done. I'm," she hesitated because here was another confession incoming that she couldn't seem to stop, "struggling a bit with the ending. When I first looked into it, I was sure it was the husband, but now I'm not sure."

She frowned, staring ahead, but aware of the levee rising up on one side, the flat marshland on the other. The sun just starting to sink bleached the color out of the ground growth.

Ahead, the edges of the swamp loomed up, unevenly lined with twisted trees and hanging moss.

"My brother had a case down here last year," she said. "One of the suspects was the Rougarou."

She grinned as Quinn glanced her way. "True story."

He chuckled. "Why does everyone need something that goes bump in the night?"

Maddie didn't have an answer and was relieved when Quinn switched the conversation back to the Calder case.

"Is the husband still alive?"

"He is. Very much so." He had money, connections, power. He'd been easy to suspect. Obvious. If it wasn't the butler, it was usually the spouse. Too bad there wasn't an unsolved case that had a butler in it. It would be fun to write that story.

"Everything I read about him," Maddie said, "made me want him to be guilty. Everyone around him did, too."

His alibi had been thin, but it had held. She'd thought she saw how he worked it, but then—and this was the truly weird part—as she began writing the story, the characters kind of came alive in her head and flowed onto the page.

It was as if she were there with them, seeing through their eyes. She couldn't say she felt sympathy for him, but his motive had begun to dissolve.

That was a strange way to put it, but that's how it had felt. And through the dissolving threads, someone else had begun to emerge.

Someone she hadn't wanted to be guilty. Someone who was supposed to be the good guy.

"But you don't think he did it, the husband?" Quinn asked, breaking into her thoughts.

"No." She sighed. "I always make myself work when the answer is kind of a cliche, but I honestly don't think he did. He was, he probably still is, a despicable, cold and calculating human being. But that's exactly why I think he didn't do it. He was capable of it, but he didn't have any reason to change the status quo."

"She was having an affair, wasn't she?"

From the side, Maddie could see the creases around his eyes that matched the frown pulling at the edges of his mouth.

"She was," Maddie admitted, "but crimes of passion need actual passion. He didn't care. At least," she added quickly, "I don't think he did."

You weren't there, she had to remind herself. She'd never met the man.

"So, who do you think did it?"

There it was. The question she didn't want to answer, the reason she couldn't write the last third of the book.

"I think it was her lover." She didn't say his name. It helped her to keep her distance. "I think he framed himself—very clumsily—so that the case against him fell apart. But yeah, I think he did it."

"Why?"

That was *the* question. Her view of him was still murky, probably because she'd built him up in her mind as another victim.

"I don't know," she admitted. "I'm about ready to put it aside and start another book. It's kind of driving me batty."

"Let's talk about another case then," Quinn suggested. "You said there were three?"

"There's the Darrow case," Maddy said, her brain reluctantly switching gears. What could she remember without her notes? It had been three years since she made her list. "Or the Merrick case."

These cases couldn't be more different. One was a blackmail case, the other might be industrial sabotage. That had been the point she'd planned to dig into.

"The Darrow case is an ugly one," Quinn said into her silence. "Blackmail, wasn't it?"

She turned to look at him.

"I told you I did some research before I came," he reminded her.

So, he had. "A lot has happened," she pointed out, her tone definitely wry.

"I didn't happen onto the Merrick case," Quinn said.

"That one is a smaller story." It was one reason she hadn't started on it, even though it definitely intrigued her.

"It was ruled an accident," Maddie said, "but there were rumors it was sabotage."

That case had another powerful person hovering in the background, but a woman this time.

The blackmail case interested her because of the smaller backdrop. Small town with small town motives. What had at first been deemed a robbery gone wrong had taken a nasty turn when the cops literally stumbled on the blackmail.

The secrets looked small to outside eyes, and blackmailers didn't get a lot of sympathy, even ones who'd masqueraded as a sweet, but nosy old lady.

It was more recent than the Ashbourne case, but only two of the blackmail victims were still alive. She could admit to herself that she hoped the killer was already dead. It made it the "safer" book to write.

The Merrick murder had more murk hanging around it. The authorities had come to believe it was a case of attempted industrial sabotage gone wrong. The three main suspects were still living, which made it tricky for her.

And then there was Quinn's case. It had been a secretary who'd been killed, if she remembered correctly. No one had been charged but the woman's employer had been suspected. Quinn's grandfather? It seemed likely.

That was the oldest of the cases. From the early 60s.

"Is anyone still alive who was involved in the Ashbourne case?" she asked, her tone carefully neutral.

He slowed to make a turn suggested by his phone's navigation.

"Only my grandmother," he said, once the truck had straightened out again.

So, it was about closure.

"That I know of," he added. "But now I wonder."

THEY MADE the rest of the drive in silence broken only when Quinn needed more specific instructions to the boat.

The road kept narrowing and he realized there was water on both sides, with narrow strips of habitation in places where the strips widened out enough.

Solid ground became more prominent, and Maddie directed him into a place that seemed to be a parking lot. There were no lines and as he turned off the engine and opened the door, the distinctive smell of swamp and seawater jumped him.

He went around and opened the door for Maddie, first helping her down, then retrieving their packages and Maddie's bags from behind the seat.

The boat she led him towards was nice looking, bigger than he'd expected. His knowledge of boats was limited to those he'd ridden in on, or egressed to, during missions.

As far as he could tell, there was an upper deck, a main deck, and probably more space below the middle deck.

It was white, well kept, and he wondered how they'd do in such a small place, even with Little Abner as a chaperone.

He didn't do casual. Even before becoming a SEAL, his respect for life and living honestly mattered. When his life had been on the line, he'd been glad he had done nothing he was ashamed of.

And, he admitted a bit wryly, as they headed for the ladder, he'd been surprised he came home. He'd been "asked" to resign for not taking the jab and he didn't regret that either.

He steadied Maddie as she climbed up the ladder, causing his throat to go bone dry, he heard footsteps and looked up in time to see Little Abner.

Of course, he wasn't at all little. He was a big man, with powerful arms and torso imperfectly covered in a muscle man shirt.

The man lifted Maddie off the ladder and set her on the deck. Without speaking, Quinn handed him the bags and packages, then climbed up to join them.

"You're Maddie," Little Abner said. He turned a gaze that could have been called cantankerous, on Quinn.

"Quinn Ellery," Quinn said.

Little Abner didn't offer his hand, so Quinn didn't either.

They sized each other up and Little Abner didn't toss him back on the dock, so he must have passed muster.

"I made some sandwiches," Little Abner finally said. "In the galley."

"That's so kind," Maddie said, "but we ate on the road. We weren't sure you'd have time to get food in."

"Well, I didn't," Little Abner said. "What you find is what you get. Gemma said you might need to spend the night?"

"Yes, if it's not too much of a problem," Maddie said.

"It's not a problem for me. I put clean sheets on the beds. There's only two rooms, so you'll," Little Abner turned to stare at Quinn, "have to sleep in the crew bunk with me."

6

Footsteps above her woke Maddie before the sun found her. She and Quinn had stayed up too late going through Maddie's files.

She respected the fact he waited until the end to look at her Ashbourne files. It was the least likely source of Maddie's problems.

If any of this was the source of her problems?

She rolled onto her back and tried to distance herself, tried to get a bird's eye view of the situation. It was easier to do first thing in the morning, not because her brain was clear and rested, but because it was never clear in the morning.

It didn't make sense but being foggy helped. Not that her brain wanted to focus on the real-life problem. It wanted to sort out the problem with her book.

She was well aware of the irony of her brain being more worried about a publishing deadline than what could be a more lethal deadline.

Was she being over dramatic?

Well, the woman had pulled a gun on her. If she played it out as if it were a book plot, she'd have been taken somewhere and met a person who wanted to know where her Fitz-D was.

And then what? It wasn't only in books that live witnesses were massively inconvenient to bad guys.

She blinked at that thought. The fog was definitely giving her some distance there.

And there was the sticking point that she was actually Fitz-D. She didn't expect that transition to go well either.

If she were more awake, she might be boggled by the idea that something she'd written, or might be writing, could freak someone out that badly.

It was true that there was no statute of limitations on murder.

However, her opinion on who did it was hardly proof.

Unless there was still proof out there that could be found if the authorities looked in the right direction?

That seemed pretty farfetched, even for her fog brain.

But she couldn't think of any reason for anyone to kill except for fear of exposure.

Could it be something she'd worked on while at the firm?

That made even less sense. She'd been a minor employee, and they didn't handle criminal cases anyway. It would be like the murderer started at the bottom of the information chain. Not unlike killing the janitor for something in the trash can.

Did she like that analogy? Not really. But she'd barely been above the janitor on the importance pole. Or not. It had definitely triggered her too-many-siblings PTSD.

Her cellphone buzzed. She picked it up. It was Frank.

"Hey," she said, aware that some morning gruffness lingered in her voice. Would he notice?

"Are you coming in today? I don't see you."

"I'm working on a case for one of my clients today."

"That's what Gideon said." Frank sounded annoyed.

Rising annoyance began to clear away the fog. That added to her annoyance.

"And you didn't believe him?"

"Well, he's sometimes wrong."

In the background, she heard Gideon say, "Hey. I'm never wrong."

In the silence that followed this, Maddie could feel Frank trying to find a pressure point to apply. There wasn't one.

"You get what you pay for, Frank," Maddie pointed out, just in case he'd forgotten she worked for zero dollars for them. And she could have used more dollars than zero. Especially if her publishing career went boom.

"Do you know when you'll be back?"

"What's the deal, Frank? I answer your phone, I greet your clients. Not exactly high-profile work."

"I have a client that needs legal advice," he admitted.

For some reason this made Maddie sit up.

"A new client?" she asked.

"Might be new."

Frank never liked to give any information if he could help. It was probably a holdover from his FBI days.

"Where are you anyway?" His tone had sharpened, as if he suddenly sensed something in a non-brother way.

"Out and about," she said.

"We could meet you somewhere."

"What kind of legal advice?"

"I don't want to talk about it over the phone," Frank said. "Could we meet you somewhere?"

"Let me get back with you on that," Maddie said, matching his evasive tone almost perfectly. When you're the youngest, with twelve siblings, that gives you twelve examples in evasiveness to learn from.

She rang off before he could protest and got up. The bathroom was a painful level of small, but she managed to clean up in record time for her.

Up on the deck, she found Quinn and Little Abner, standing in front of an easel with a whiteboard. They both had their feet planted, their arms crossed over their chests and their gazes fixed on the board.

Maddie came forward and saw that one of them had made columns for the four cases they'd talked about last night.

It was kind of cute, though she did wonder how Little Abner had ended up on their team.

They hadn't noticed her yet, so she used the time to study the board herself. It was interesting seeing the data like this. She worked completely on her computer. It was faster, in her opinion, and necessary because she couldn't read her own handwriting.

This board was very legible and it had the basic suspects. The Ashbourne column was on the scarce side, since only one person from that time was still alive.

She studied each column, finding this new way of presenting the facts was a perspective shift. It had only the most basic facts, but now her memory filled in details.

Witness statements. Time of death and alibis. When she started the book, she'd look at the crime scene photos to get a sense of movement and flow, but it was her least favorite part. She didn't like seeing dead people. Her thing was solving puzzles.

And her strength was figuring people out, somehow seeing what their motives were without being told. She didn't know if Zach or any of her siblings knew it, but she'd meet someone, and she could sense or see if they were friend or enemy. Or annoying, though that probably wasn't a super power, just common sense.

Now, the board felt like seeing a skeleton without the meat.

They'd gone over it all last night until her brain felt like exploding, but now...something was missing. Or had she missed something?

But for which case?

She must have made a small sound because Quinn spun around.

"Are you all right?"

"Yes, probably," she said. "I'm just..." She waved her arms around.

"Too much incoming?" His grin was sympathetic.

He was a very nice man.

"Frank called me this morning. He suddenly has a client who needs legal advice." She hadn't realized her brain had circled back to that until she said the words. She directed a look at Quinn, then at Little Abner. "Am I getting paranoid?"

QUINN FELT like his thoughts were as twisty as the road they followed back to New Orleans.

Were they being paranoid? On the one hand, what sense did it make to try to get to Maddie through her brother? It wasn't like they could kill everyone.

Was it just a coincidence? The person could actually need legal advice. Or, like the woman who had tried to snatch Maddie's bag and the other woman who had held her up in the john, this one could have been hired to smoke Maddie out of hiding.

Even if someone had tried to use her family to track her down, it would be time consuming. Very time consuming. Twelve siblings, some of them married. It would have taken a while to uncover the link to the boat.

Now, he wouldn't have liked to be found there. Too few

escape routes. But it had been a great place to pause and regroup. He'd learned a lot about the cases.

Except for who Maddie thought was the killer in his grandfather's case.

It had been an interesting exercise in learning how her mind worked. She'd have been a great tactician for his SEAL team.

He glanced at her, noting the purse of her lips as she pondered their next step.

"I have to give Frank some time to get his client," she said. "New Orleans is a pretty compact city on paper, but it's a mare's nest to drive through."

He couldn't argue with that. Streets going the wrong direction. The bridge to the West Bank going due East. So much wrong.

"Do you think you should be with me or close by? I can't decide which would be better."

"I'm thinking on that myself," he admitted. He felt a strange desire not to let her get too far away from him. But if he was at the table, he wouldn't be able to see if anyone was taking an interest in her. "I should probably take a position where I can see more. Maybe see what our options are when we get there?"

"We need to pick a spot, too. What do you need?"

"A place that will be quiet enough for a talk, I suppose." He thought about it. "Easy egress if things get dicey. Privacy but not too much privacy."

"We could go for private," Maddie offered. "My dad's house or Sarah's place. But I'd feel guilty if I were pulling danger into their orbit."

"There's the office," Quinn pointed out.

She made a face. He didn't blame her. It felt like they'd been lucky to get out of there the last time.

"Maybe we're over thinking this."

He gave an agreeing shrug. "Could be." He thought for a moment. "Why don't you ask your brother to pick the place?"

Maddie grinned. "Good idea. And he'll have to pay the bill."

IN TYPICAL FRANK FASHION, he'd picked a place with good food, discreetly upscale in design, and middle-of-the-road pricing.

Maddie knew all of this because it used to be in her price range.

She checked her phone. "They are this way."

She led the way through the carefully spaced tables toward a booth in the back. Frank was visible, but his companion was not. She angled right, so they could approach from the side and give Quinn a chance to see who was with Frank.

Quinn gave a murmur she took to be approval and then she got her first, good look at Frank's client.

She stopped in shock and Quinn did not bump into her. She glanced back. It wasn't because of good reflexes. He looked as shocked as she felt. She frowned. No, he was definitely more shocked.

She turned her attention and her gaze back to the table. Neither of them had noticed them yet. They were both studying large menus.

Old lady.

Yeah, she was old, but still sturdy, her back so straight, Maddie winced and then checked her own shoulders. Her hair was white and fluffed around her face like a halo. She had a sweet, fluffy face, but her eyes were shrewd.

Maddie bet the old lady's clothes were what she wore to church. The neck of her dress was rimmed with off-white lace that had probably been white at some point. It looked as aged as its wearer.

Maddie inhaled, half expecting to find the old lady's vintage scent in the air, instead of a rich cocktail of spices that made her mouth water.

Breakfast had been lean, and on the sad side.

She felt warmth as Quinn stepped in close to her.

"I wasn't expecting..." she began.

"That's my," she thought he swallowed hard, "my grandmother."

QUINN NUDGED MADDIE GENTLY FORWARD, his hand cupping her elbow. He still felt the tremors of shock from his disclosure, but her face was normal.

Her brother glanced their way and slid out to greet her.

"Maddie." His gaze moved past her to Quinn, but he knew how to maintain a poker face.

"Frank." Maddie's tone was exquisitely neutral.

Quinn mentally winced. It was not his custom to use the word "exquisitely" either out loud or inside his head.

His grandmother's gaze was a laser on him. He resisted the urge to shuffle his feet and hang his head. There was no way to quantify how bad he did not want to say it. But he had to. It was his obligation as a grandson.

"Gammie."

"Well," his Gammie said, her huff a familiar one. It had preceded every dressing down she'd ever given him. He felt the years falling off, leaving him about ten. "Quinnie."

He winced. He couldn't help it.

Her gaze flicked to Maddie and grew speculative. It didn't make him feel any better. Gammie was intensely interested in the lives of all her grandchildren. This interest included their love lives. How she wielded such power still baffled him.

"This is my sister Maddie, Mrs. Ashbourne." If Frank sensed tension, it didn't interfere with his manners. "Maddie, this is Mrs. Ashbourne."

Maddie extended her hand, let the Gammie's claw-like hand with its paper-thin white skin close around it. This blocked his view of Gammie. He didn't mind that one bit.

"It's nice to meet you, ma'am," Maddie said.

"Call me Gammie," his grandmother told her.

Quinn wanted to sit down and put his face in his hands. Into the silence, Maddie said, "Gammie."

Quinn was impressed. Maddie didn't hesitate over the name and there was no sign of humor in her voice.

"You could have saved me a trip if I'd known you'd already met this gal." Gammie's tone was measured, a concession Quinn was sure, to their public location. Though she could easily rip him a new one without raising her voice.

Frank broke in smoothly, "Mrs. Ashbourne has been telling me something interesting, Maddie. I guess I missed the memo about you becoming a literary agent?"

"Literary lawyer," Maddie corrected.

"Literary lawyer," Frank said smoothly, "for..."

His voice died. He didn't want to say the author's name. No one did. Saying it just made you feel like you'd wandered into a weird comedy.

"S.C. Fitz-Dankworthington," Maddie said.

She'd probably had a lot of practice saying it. Quinn noted that Gammie's approving expression deepened and shifted from one foot to the other. The fact that he liked Maddie a lot more than he wanted to, didn't stop the instinctive feeling of wanting to back slowly away from both women. He quelled it. He and Maddie weren't on a date, and he was a grown man.

A grown man who felt ten years old, but a grown man. Who'd been a SEAL. He could do this.

"Maybe we should all sit down," Maddie said. "I believe Gammie wants legal advice from me?"

Frank indicated Maddie should sit on his side of the table. Gammie slid over and patted the bench next to her.

At least she'd left him an escape route. He was old enough now to outrun her.

"I don't want legal advice," Gammie said. She shot Frank a look. "I said that so you'd let me talk to this little gal."

"You wanted to talk to Maddie..." Frank said.

"Actually, I really want to talk to that Fitz something or other. I want to meet him."

He didn't have to see Gammie's face to know from personal experience the power of the look she currently directed at Maddie. It would be speculative, but also compelling. Gammie's gaze was legendary among the cousins.

But Maddie was the youngest of thirteen. She didn't disappoint.

"Mr. Fitz-Dankworthington isn't writing a book about your family, ma'am."

It was a smart move not to avail herself of the permission to call her Gammie at this moment.

"Well why not?"

Quinn blinked. So did Maddie. Frank might have winced.

"Why...not?" Maddie repeated.

"Isn't my family murder good enough for you?"

Maddie's mouth moved. "Your family murder is...great. Fascinating even."

"Dang right it is."

Quinn risked a glance at Gammie. Oh yeah, she had the look. But the motive behind the look? Nothing in his training had prepared him for this.

He felt her elbow dig into his ribs.

"Isn't that why you're here? To ask her about our murder?"

"Well, yes," Quinn said. He sounded normal. That was good. "And," he started to add, but stopped. He doubted that Gammie knew about the murder of the other Fitz-Dankworthington. "I was curious," he said.

Gammie angled to look at him.

"Curious."

"Curious," he insisted.

"Hmmm."

Gammie straightened her body and redirected her gaze to Maddie.

"So, if our murder is *fascinating* why isn't your author writing about it?"

"It's on his list." Her voice had lost some of its evenness.

"On his list." Gammie leaned back, crossing her arms over her thin chest. "He needs to move it up his list."

Maddie opened her mouth. Closed it. "That, he..."

"I want to talk to him."

Despite his own inner squirming, Quinn might have been enjoying this.

"As Mr. Fitz..."

"Humph."

Maddie glanced at Frank. Quinn wished he wasn't here, too. He made it hard for Maddie to confess. He could have told her it was pointless, but he didn't want to call attention to himself.

He'd learned how to keep quiet, and he brought all his skill to bear.

Gammie swung around again.

"You think it's funny?"

"No ma'am." He knew when to deploy a "ma'am" as well as Maddie.

A waitress approached their table and veered off when Gammie sent her a look.

Maddie absorbed the return of Gammie's attention like a

trooper, Quinn thought. She bit her lip, then leaned forward just a bit. She almost rested her elbows on the table, but hastily lowered them to her lap.

"The thing is, ma'am, an author, my client, considers a lot of factors when choosing what story to write."

"Indeed?" Gammie's voice was quiet. Too quiet.

"Mr. FitzDankingworth has to look at, well, multiple suspects and he has a lot of detail to sift through. The case is unsolved and interesting, but there's not a lot there for him to work with."

Gammie's gaze narrowed and the clash of gazes was dang near epic. Quinn noticed Frank studied the menu as if it held the secret to life.

"I want to meet him."

"I can't do that."

Quinn felt a tremor in his force.

"It's because of situations like this one that he guards his privacy. He needs emotional distance and...and..."

"I see," Gammie said.

Quinn had a bad feeling she did see.

Maddie didn't flinch, but Quinn thought her pupils dilated.

Gammie's gaze shifted just slightly to Frank and then she leaned back.

"We should order."

Quinn noted that Maddie's shoulders relaxed ever so slightly. So did his.

It wasn't over, but it was a reprieve. He wanted a reprieve. He just didn't know how it helped. He had no idea what Gammie was up to.

FRANK PAID the bill with less reluctance than was usual for him.

"If you don't need me, I should get back to the office," he said.

It was obvious that no one needed him or wanted him, Maddie thought ruefully. Unlike Alex, Frank liked to avoid messes with emotional overtones. He probably wouldn't even ask her later what it was about. Or about her literary attorney gig.

Of course, Alex didn't like all the emotion either, but he would wade in with the conviction that he could weed out the emotion and get to the essential problem. His wife, Nell, was helping him deal with that delusion. But even she couldn't completely shut down the Big Brother-itis.

Maddie slid out so Frank could leave. She stood watching him. He moved well and without hurry, but she knew he wouldn't relax until he was out of sight. If she had a favorite brother—which of course she didn't—it was probably Frank because she could count on him to be the least curious about her life.

When they were alone, Maddie perched on the edge of the seat and waited, trying not to wilt under the force of Gammie's gaze. She only had Zach to judge the force of parental gazes. Both her grandparents had died before she was born.

She figured Gammie wielded some power in the family, based on *Quinnie's* reaction to her. If Gammie hadn't been watching her, Maddie might have grinned at that memory.

"I want that fella to come to my house," Gammie said finally —and with an air of finality. "I was there." She looked at Quinn. "I was expecting your mama, so...well, there might be more to the story that could be told."

Maddie felt cold run down her back. Quinn's whole body stilled with what felt like menace.

A man, his neighbor had died, Maddie reminded herself. And this was his grandmother.

"I read about that Fitz-whatever who was killed and I thought..." she stopped. "But then it turns out he wasn't the one who wrote the books. And that made me wonder some more."

She turned abruptly and put her hand on Quinn's arm. It was so small against his, so frail and claw-like.

"I might be the only left who knows some things, Quinnie."

Maddie didn't have to be the daughter of a cop to know that wasn't a good thing.

Both Quinn and his Gammie turned her way again. Was it the light that made it seem like they had the same expression in their eyes.

Quinn, because he knew. Gammie because she didn't know.

She gave a sigh and saw the edge of Quinn's mouth quirk up.

She put her elbow on the table and rubbed her temple. Gammie might have squeaked at this breach of etiquette, but Maddie didn't care. Was it just yesterday that her life started to go off the careful track she'd been steering it down?

Could this old lady and the attempted assaults be related? It defied logic, but then instinct often did. *There is more that could be told.*

The author in her felt a stirring, too.

She lowered her arm and sat up straight, her hands clasped in her lap as if she were a schoolgirl.

"There is something you need to know, ma'am," Maddie said. "There isn't a Mr. Fitz-Dankworthington. That's a pen name."

"What a shock," Gammie said dryly. "I still want to meet him."

"You have met him," Maddie fumbled, feeling like she was back in law school facing her first teacher. "I mean, I'm him. I'm her. I wrote the books."

Gammie leaned back, nothing even close to surprise in her lined face. "I did wonder if a woman had written them."

"Did you?" Quinn actually looked surprised.

Gammie ignored him. "Are you going to help me?"

"By help you..." Maddie probed carefully.

"Help me solve the murder. What else did you think I wanted?"

World peace, Maddie wanted to say. She didn't. Zach had raised her to not be a fool or to sass her elders.

"I can't promise you I can figure it out," Maddie said.

Gammie just looked at her.

"I can try," she said. She looked at Quinn for help. Or for something.

"You could be in danger, Gammie," he said. Now he covered her hand with his. "Someone has already tried to find Fitz-whatever."

Gammie looked at him, her faded eyes glinting with amusement. "I'm ninety years old, Quinnie."

"I know, but..."

"It's time the truth came out. I owe that to my friend."

My friend.

Etta Mae Johnson, a black housekeeper, had been murdered in 1963. But this old lady had called her my friend.

Even if this wasn't *the* case that was complicating her life, she knew she had to try to figure this out for Gammie.

"Okay," Maddie said. "Let's do this."

She'd have laughed as they both looked at Quinn for the next step—but she didn't dare.

"I guess we go to Gammie's," he said.

Quinnie. Gammie. Man, she wished she knew him better. That was some fertile comedic ground.

7

A neighbor had found Gammie a ride to New Orleans, so the only problem he had was getting Gammie up into his truck without assaulting her dignity. He mostly avoided looking at Maddie. He could remind himself all day that he was a former SEAL, but she'd heard his *Gammie* call him *Quinnie*. He didn't know how to come back from that.

At least Gammie was still Gammie. She filled what would have been a silence, telling Maddie about herself, about who'd she been in 1963.

He knew all the facts, but it felt odd hearing them from her.

"I was expecting my youngest child that year. Now we know what having five kids does to a gal, but I just knew this one was harder than the others. And the heat." She paused. "I'll always remember the heat."

Quinn knew her gaze would be distant now, as she looked back into her memories, unwrapping them slowly and carefully. His grandfather had been a storyteller, but Gammie was a memory teller. People might not know the difference, but he did. Not that he could explain it. It just was.

Beside him, Gammie was rubbing her middle as if his mother were still there, under her heart.

"You probably can't imagine what it was like then. I always knew it was wrong, what people did to blacks." She sighed. "But I didn't talk about it. I knew, without being told, what it would do to our *standing*." She huffed. "I was young, but I don't excuse myself. You can believe me or not, but I never...my Walter made better money than some, but it was still a stretch for us to hire Etta Mae. She was my friend. She'd been my friend from the first time we met playing in the woods."

She fell silent for a while, and Quinn knew these memories were for her.

"She was going to have to leave to find work. Her mama was sick. Me and Walter talked it over. People thought they knew why we hired her. They didn't know anything. We worked side by side in the house and she helped Walter with his bookkeeping. She was that smart. She could have gone to college. She should have. Her mama died early that year. I've always been glad she didn't live to see..."

Gammie's voice trailed off again. She took a deep, sighing breath.

"She was going to leave, to move North with...someone. She almost made it."

For a long time, she didn't speak, and Quinn began to wonder if she'd tired herself out. Or had gotten lost in the past.

"People thought it was my Walter she was meeting. I knew better. I always knew better. That had to be enough. It mostly was enough, us both knowing the truth. It bothered the kids when they got older. Some believed me when I said it wasn't true. Some, not so much. That hurt him. We maybe could have fixed it, but he wouldn't. The past is the past, he'd tell me."

Was it?

Quinn glanced over and met Maddie's gaze across his Gammie's head.

"They say the truth will set you free, but if it's just half the truth?" She sighed again.

He looked back at the road. "You're tiring yourself out," he said. "Leave it until we get you home."

"Yes," Gammie said. "When I get home."

She must have closed her eyes, because she sagged softly against Maddie, who steadied her with a gentle touch.

GAMMIE'S HOUSE WAS CHARMING, Maddie decided. Set on a corner lot, it was white trim and red brick with a wraparound porch and big, deep windows. Several trees in the yard shaded portions of the house and the gnome-like cypress knees poked up out of an otherwise nice lawn.

Quinn pulled around the back between the house and what had probably been a garage or maybe even a stable. It didn't seem to be either anymore. Gammie' confirmed her guess.

"That's Walter's office, where it happened."

She led them past it, unlocking the back door into a kitchen that was almost a vintage lover's delight. Low counters and cabinets that reached to a ceiling higher than Maddie could get at. A small stove and a couple of closets. The living room and dining room area had wood floors and furniture that she'd have called battered in any other house.

It was obvious that Gammie was still in there fighting against time and dust and starting to lose.

There was a bedroom and bathroom off the living area and, she was informed, two bedrooms and a bath upstairs. She realized that one of the closets in the kitchen was actually narrow stairs. The bedrooms were tucked under slanting eaves—as was the shower in the bathroom. It was small enough to give her claustrophobia. She couldn't see how Quinn would manage it.

He gave her a rueful shrug when she looked from him to the shower.

"It used to be easier," he admitted. He lowered his voice. "I'm surprised she's letting us both sleep up here."

Maddie shifted her weight to one foot and the floor creaked.

"There is that," he admitted with a low chuckle.

The small, humorous moment eased something tight in her chest and she felt better able to go back downstairs. Would Gammie continue her story tonight? And she realized there was a gap in her knowledge. What was Gammie's first name? She didn't remember seeing it in the information she had on the Ashbourne case. And that was interesting.

And was she surprised that in 1963, the police file might have been scrubbed a little? Or a lot?

After the events of the last few days, she didn't much like the wide low windows on two sides of the living area. It felt a lot like being a fish in a bowl.

Did Quinn seem uneasy, too? He didn't say anything as he helped Gammie settle into what was obviously her chair. There was a table on one side, its top scattered with old lady things like glasses lozenges, a magazine and television remote. It also had a footstool positioned just right in front of it. Lace doilies covered both arms and the back where Gammie's head now rested.

It was all fading gently and she wondered what it had been like when her kids were running around it. Zach's house was definitely the worse for wear after the tornado of thirteen passing through it.

She studied it, feeling the sense of place enveloping her in a sharper way than was usual. It wasn't fancy, despite the kind of upscale look of the exterior. She'd seen houses similar to this one, resting between "getting along" and "fancy." It wasn't quite in the middle for the rest of the world, but in this little town? It could have passed for upper middle.

Upper middle would be a precarious place for someone who befriended a black woman in the 60s. And for a young, pregnant woman with other small children? She could see why Gammie hadn't spoken up—and why she still felt guilt about it.

The money might have gotten easier with time, but now Maddie felt the lingering scent of old regret.

She wandered the room, studying the photographs on the walls. "Is this your husband?" she asked over her shoulder.

"That's him." Gammie's voice turned tender.

"He was nice looking." Was that appropriate to say?

"That he was," Gammie said. "He was a good man. A brave man." A pause. "Quinn takes after him."

Quinn made a small sound and Maddie bit her lower lip. If Gammie were matchmaking things could get interesting. It was odd, though, that she felt no urge to make a discreet, but hurried exit. Granted, that would be hard without wheels. But Quinn wasn't fleeing either. Was it just his Gammie's story keeping him in place?

"I don't go into the office, haven't since that day."

The abrupt change in tone caught Maddie by surprise. She spun around.

"You know the basic story?"

Maddie nodded. Both police and newspaper reports at the time. The police report had been sparse. The newspapers, depending on which, were either on the lurid side or equally discreet. But based on what Quinn had told her—confirmed by Gammie—a taint on their family had lingered.

People had believed Walter and Etta Mae had been having an affair.

There'd been nothing to connect Walter to the murder—at least nothing that couldn't be explained away as him using his own office. Reading between the lines, officials had decided Etta Mae had interrupted a burglar. She'd died from a single blow to the head. There were some signs she'd put up a struggle.

The office had been ransacked. Depending on point of view, it was either proof of an outside intruder or a clever way to hide a crime.

Maddie couldn't even explain to herself why this case had caught her eye. She never could. Sometimes insight was blinding and so obvious she couldn't believe it had been missed. Other times it was a twitch between her shoulder blades.

This case had been a twitch.

"Here's the key, if you want to see it."

Maddie exchanged a look with Quinn, but he just nodded when he accepted the key and led them back through the kitchen and outside.

"You don't have to do this," he said, without looking at her. "I had no idea."

"I don't suppose you did," she said, her tone neutral. "I've never actually been in a real crime scene."

Just when had that door been locked? It was an office. Surely it hadn't been left like that.

Quinn reached out to insert the key and the door swung open. He glanced back at her, then gently pushed the door.

The smell of antiseptic wafted out the opening.

QUINN PULLED out his phone and used its flashlight to see as much as he could from the doorway, but the smell of cleaning solution told him what he'd find.

Nothing.

"That," Maddie said, peering around him, "is an unusual break in."

He glanced down at her and felt his shoulder brush against something. A wire. He tackled Maddie to the side, covering her with his body as heat flashed out of the doorway they'd been standing in.

He cautiously lifted his head. The bomb had been low yield, precise. A discreet whump. No fire and the walls were still standing, though the glass from the single window was gone. He was glad he'd gone this way and not toward it. He hated trying to get glass fragments off his clothes.

He rolled off Maddie and lay for a minute looking up at the sky.

"If they were going to blow it up, why clean it?" Maddie asked.

He turned his head. She'd rolled onto her back, too. She'd also tucked her hands behind her head and seemed to be studying a cloud drifting slowly past their patch of sky. It was weird to still catch hints of cleaning solution mingled with the acrid smell of explosive.

He gave a half shrug. Did this mean that his family murder was the source of all their problems? Or was someone playing with them? SEALs were trained to adapt, to adjust to rapidly changing circumstances, but war still had a certain logic to it.

The enemy tried to trap and/or kill you.

You tried to stop them trapping and/or killing you. And you tried to kill them if your orders allowed it.

These simple truths took some of the randomness from what he'd done.

"If you were writing this story..." he began slowly.

"I would get laughed out of...everywhere. Too unbelievable."

She was silent for a few minutes. Quinn didn't mind. After all the back and forth and disclosures of the last two days, it was nice to stop.

"That was my first explosion," she said, finally. "So, the fact that it feels a bit like a nothing burger might not be relevant." A pause. "My ears aren't even ringing."

"Mine aren't either," Quinn said. He listened for the warning crackle of fire, but all he picked up was the distant sound of cars. A short, sharp dog bark. Not even any insects in close proximity.

He'd been this quiet before out on missions. What was different was the sense of peace. Okay, that was a bit nuts just a few minutes after the bomb went off. But as she'd pointed out, it was a nothing burger bomb.

Maddie rolled to her side, her elbow propped to support her head. "I'm hungry."

Quinn tipped his head. There was a sound. His stomach growling. He rolled to his feet and held out a hand to her. "I am, too."

She came up easily with his help, landing within smelling distance. He inhaled her scent, felt a deep-seated rightness, a feeling of coming home after a long journey. His sense of her closeness was heightened by his hand holding hers. Had he ever held a woman's hand like this? He didn't think so. He didn't want to stop. That was also new.

He met her gaze. Her head was tipped to the side, her gaze curious. Did she feel it, too? He couldn't tell. He didn't want to look away or even speak.

Her stomach growled and then his did.

They both laughed and the moment dissipated like morning mist.

Except that somehow, he found he was still holding her hand as they went back to the house.

8

Maddie nibbled at her sandwich, trying very hard not to hear what Quinn and the local police were talking about. She needed to *think*. The sound of their voices was like a mosquito buzzing in her ear.

The doorway darkened. Maddie looked up. It was Gammie.

She closed the door, which lowered the sound to Maddie's relief. Maddie started to rise, but she waved her back to her seat, then sat down opposite her. Maddie noticed she rested her elbows on the table, but admitted she might need the support. Earlier, she'd appeared engaged and interested, definitely resolute. Now she was a tired, bewildered old lady.

She'd unleashed the whirlwind and changed the tenor of her life. Maddie felt fellow sympathy for her. A different whirlwind but becoming an author and her own agent had definitely changed Maddie's life. And in some weird way it had blown her here.

She started to pick up her sandwich, but instead she pushed the plate to one side and studied the old lady.

"In 1963, interracial marriage wasn't just illegal. It was also illegal for anyone to assist in or promote it."

Gammie met Maddie's gaze without flinching. "Yes."

"So, what happened to the husband?" The spouse or boyfriend was usually looked at first in a homicide, but they hadn't known about the husband.

"I don't know," Gammie said. "I mean," she corrected, "I heard he'd left town. I never saw him after…"

She stopped and a wry smile edged her mouth. "I went into labor the day after the murder. I was—happy—to be distracted."

"He didn't go to her funeral?" Maddie frowned.

"I was informed I wasn't welcome at the funeral," Gammie said.

"I thought her mother…"

"She had other family."

Maddie considered this. "Was there a man in that community who liked her?"

Gammie nodded. "He left a few years later. Don't know what happened to him."

What would the police have done with this information back then, aside from arresting Gammie and her husband? But the more current question was: what might they do with this information now? Whoever had killed Etta Mae could still be charged and convicted—if they could find evidence after all this time.

Could be whoever was doing this was more worried about being branded a killer, rather than arrested.

The nothing burger bombing could have been an attempt to destroy evidence, or a sign of fear that there might still be evidence there.

"Can you think of anything that might have still been in there that someone would want to destroy?"

"The only one who could answer that question was my husband."

And the murderer. Maddie couldn't help wondering if her husband had been innocent. She was, after all, a lawyer.

"Why did you come to me, ma'am? What is it you want?"

"I want the truth."

Did she? "What if you don't like what I find? What if I can't?"

Maddie respected Gammie for pausing to consider these questions.

Then Gammie leaned forward, holding Maddie with her formidable gaze. She could even teach Zach some things about hard gazing.

"Even if you find out it was my husband, I want to know. And if you can't?" She shrugged. "At least I tried. For Etta Mae."

QUINN DIDN'T BLAME the cop for being skeptical of his story. Hearing him say it out loud? He was skeptical of it. Of course he'd left things out. How could he explain why he'd contacted Maddie? He'd lived next door to a man who had been murdered, then come here and almost been blown up? So, he'd stepped lightly across the tricky details.

Maddie had come here to help his grandmother with a legal matter, an old legal matter relating to his grandfather. His grandmother had suggested there might be information in the old office. It had clearly been broken into, and he'd realized there was a trip wire and then boom. He hadn't mentioned the smell of cleaning fluid.

The story was already thin without that.

But he had no right to out Maddie as an author. And none of it made sense to them. How could he make it make sense to this cop who was clearly out of his depth?

"We'll have to get a team from the Parish Sheriff's office to go over the scene," the cop finally said.

"I appreciate you coming out and checking," Quinn said. He gave the man a bland look. "Do you think my grandmother is safe?"

"Would she have gone in there on her own?" the man asked.

"I'd say no, but if she saw the door ajar, I guess she might have checked it." Quinn felt a stab of worry at this thought. Had his grandmother been the target? They'd assumed it was them, but if Gammie hadn't come to find them... "I don't like it," he admitted.

"I don't either. Your Gammie is respected in these parts."

At least he hadn't said "feared."

"She might want to stay with family until we get this sorted out."

"I'll make some calls," Quinn said. "I'll try to figure out a way to persuade Gammie to do it."

The cop chuckled. "Good luck with that."

He didn't say what they were both thinking. She was a stubborn old bird. She was ninety and probably shouldn't be living alone, but no one'd had the courage to suggest she move out. Lucky for them, she'd given up driving on her own volition. She'd even sold her car to get rid of the temptation to just run a quick errand.

Of course, her "volition" had been helped when she drove the wrong way down the main street and bumped up on the curb, almost running down the mayor, but as Gammie liked to say, that was just a detail.

He shook hands with the cop and showed him out, watching him walk slowly to his patrol car. He felt for him. He didn't know what to do next either.

His Gammie cleared her throat behind him, and he spun around. Maddie stood behind her, her gaze worried.

"I need you to collect all the albums, Quinnie. The picture albums," she added.

What, she thought he'd think she wanted record albums? Did Gammie even have a record player anymore?

"Sure," he said. He hesitated. "He's taped off the scene and is going to call a forensic team from the Parish Sheriff's Office."

"He has no idea what to do, does he?" Gammie sounded stringent, but her face looked drawn with gray edges.

"No."

"What did you tell him?"

"As little as possible," Quinn admitted.

Gammie gave an approving nod. "No sense confusing the boy. He's grown a bit since I saw him last. I heard he got his badge. Go on, get going."

Quinn forgave the sharpness in her tone. She was worried, too.

～

MADDIE MIGHT HAVE BEEN RELIEVED when the insistent whine of her cellphone took her away from the album browsing. Slightly blurry pictures of people she didn't know and would never know didn't really float her boat.

That it was Gideon calling was less happy making.

"Hey," she said, walking into the other room as she spoke.

"Maddie? Where are you?"

Gideon didn't sound worried. She knew all the tones of all the brothers. Gideon was annoyed.

"I'm helping a client," Maddie said. "Didn't Frank tell you?"

"I haven't seen Frank."

The silence that followed this also didn't surprise her. It was tough to be annoyed with her when they didn't pay her. So far it was working out better than she'd expected.

"I checked your schedule this morning," she offered as a palliative.

"It's not about me," Gideon sounded almost smug, but quickly reverted to annoyed. "These people keep showing up wanting to see you."

"People?"

"Well, three people. One of them was a cop from Plonkville." His tone seemed to indicate that Plonkville shouldn't have or need a cop. But if it had to have one, it should keep its cops confined to Plonkville.

Maddie blinked. That was...odd.

"And the other two?"

She heard the rustling of paper and then the pause while he tried to figure out what he'd written down.

"Someone named Darrow." Another pause, then he must have given up figuring out the first name. "I'll text you the phone number. The other was Matrix, no Merrick. I'll send you that number, too."

"Thank you," Maddie said. She almost sighed. Maybe she shouldn't have been so quick to declare her S. C. Fitz-Dankworthington alive.

"When will you be back?"

He took care to keep his tone neutral this time. If he admitted he needed her, she might start asking for a salary.

This made her grin.

"If I'm not in today, I'll be in tomorrow," she decided. If there'd been something to see or learn here, it had been exploded, leaving only Gammie. The old lady was portable. Had Quinn been thinking about where to stash his grandmother to keep her safe?

Probably, she decided.

She finished her call with Gideon and sank down on a stool. She'd learned some things here, no question, but were they the right things?

The same instincts that brought her here were now telling

her she needed to leave. The only way to visit the sites of either the Darrow or Merrick murders was by plane.

Her phone pinged with an incoming text, and she glanced down. The promised phone numbers.

She pursed her lips, thinking. She didn't feel an urgency to call either of them.

What were the odds that three of her possible book ideas had stirred up—she didn't know what to call the situation she currently found herself in.

It had overtones of a quagmire, in that she felt kind of stuck, but she wasn't actually stuck. At least, if Quinn took her back to town, she wouldn't be stuck. Or she could rent a car.

She felt her credit card wince at this thought.

She had just made up her mind to go ask Quinn to take her back to New Orleans, when he pushed open the door, halting in the frame.

Did he know how nice he looked framed like that?

"I think we should head back to New Orleans," he said. "I need to find a safe place for...my grandmother, but I'd like her to be close if we need to talk to her."

He hadn't asked her for a suggestion, but she found herself producing one.

"Zach, my dad could probably put her up. Becca, his wife, is super nice."

Maddie was probably the sibling with the least issues with Becca, since she'd been very young when her mother died.

He hesitated.

"He's an ex-cop," she reminded him, by way of comfort. "Thirteen kids who all survived their childhood."

"True." He grinned tiredly. "Thanks. I'll get Gam—my grandmother moving."

Interesting that he felt the same undercurrent of urgency that she did.

He returned in a few minutes, and she decided to use the alone time to update him on her calls.

"I'm guessing you know your local cops?" she asked when she'd finished.

Quinn's face wore a frown that held a hint of increased worry. His poker face appeared to be fraying as fast as hers. But he nodded.

"I talked to him the day I found Sol's body."

"What I don't understand is why he came to the office. He had my number." It was her turn to frown. "And the others. I mean, you obviously connected my number to the office, how had he done that, she wondered, "but I have a post office box for my business address."

"I know," he said. "I went to the office, hoping someone there could help me find you. And when I saw you, I took a chance."

For the first time since she'd met him, Maddie felt like he'd held something back. Had he perhaps used some channels he shouldn't have? She let it pass. For now.

"I can get a cop tracking down that address," Maddie said, "but the other two? How easy was it for you to find the connection between me and Gideon? Baker isn't that unusual of a name."

"No," Quinn agreed. "But as you pointed out, your family is rather steeped in law enforcement."

Before Maddie could decide whether to dive deeper into this statement, Gammie appeared.

"My bag is on the bed. Where am I going?"

Maddie had expected her to look unhappy, but the old lady had a gleam in her eyes and two spots of color on her pale, crepey skin.

"Let me call my dad," she said. "I'm pretty sure he'll be happy for you to visit."

Okay, that was stretching the truth. What Zach would be

happy about was getting to be in her muddle and offer advice. Lots of advice.

9

N o one spoke much as Quinn steered his truck back to New Orleans. Gammie was much more tired than she was let on, but when he asked her if she was okay, she'd responded with her usual spunk.

"Tired doesn't kill you."

Quinn wasn't sure that was true of a woman her age, but he wasn't stupid enough to say it to her.

They stopped once for food and gas, and it was on the late side by the time he'd followed Maddie's directions to her father's house.

He couldn't tell much about it. The streetlamp's light didn't meet up with the porch light gleaming at the end of the driveway.

He got out and came around, helping both women to clamber down. Even Maddie seemed a bit stiff, but she walked it off as she led the way toward that light.

Her father was an older version of both Gideon and Frank. A much older version, but his eyes were still keen and alert. Quinn would have known him for a cop without being told.

Becca was like a warm fire in the small, rather battered looking kitchen.

Gammie took to her immediately and went without hesitation to get settled in.

That left he, Maddie, and her father alone in the kitchen. Her father's gaze affected him almost like a Gammie gaze. No, that wasn't quite right. More like a drill sergeant's.

Unconsciously, he straightened his shoulders and then regretted it when a satisfied gleam shot out of the old man's eyes.

"So," her dad said, "I think you need to tell me what's going on."

IT DIDN'T TAKE THAT LONG for Maddie to give Zach the basic facts, but it took every inch of her training as a lawyer not to falter or look away.

At least Quinn already knew her guilty secret.

And Zach wouldn't call her out for keeping secrets in front of Quinn. He's the one her brothers had learned that important life lesson from.

She finished all the details, holding nothing back except the fact that she'd just barely met Quinn. She had a feeling it would come up at some point, but for now Zach was considering all the details she'd tossed his way.

"I'm feeling pretty stumped right now," Maddie admitted, now playing the daughter card. "I have too many..."

"You should have been a cop," Zach said when she'd trailed off. "You've got a good brain."

"I..." she began defensively, then stopped. He'd never actually said she should be a cop, just that she shouldn't be a lawyer. Zach wasn't a huge proponent of his daughters being in high-risk jobs. He'd just given her a huge compliment. "I guess I take after my dad," she said instead.

Zach gave her a grim smile. His gaze traveled between them. "You should both rest, too. Let me think on it, sleep on it. Maybe something will pop out to me."

Maddie looked at Quinn. Did he have a place to stay?

"He can have the couch," Zach said. "It's almost long enough."

"Thank you, sir," Quinn said, his voice carefully respectful.

Maddie might be impressed. Had he known it was a test of sorts? She glanced at Quinn, but his face was carefully bland. He probably didn't dare have any expression in front of Zach.

"I'll get you a pillow and some blankets," Maddie said. As she passed her dad, she stopped to give him a hug, felt him hold her for an extra few seconds.

He was worried.

Well, so was she.

THE COUCH WASN'T AS bad as Quinn had expected it to be. It was clear it had been used a lot, but was one of those couches that got more comfortable the worse they looked.

He lay on his back, his hands clasped behind his head and did a mental post-mission assessment.

As a SEAL, it was what he'd done after every mission. Studied it for opportunities missed, or areas he hadn't noted at the time. While this situation wasn't as fast moving as a SEAL operation, it hadn't been slow either.

Two days.

And a wide variety of threats.

He closed his eyes, visualizing the board they'd created on the boat. What had they missed?

He slipped into sleep before he found anything.

THE NEXT MORNING, Maddie found Gammie and Becca chatting amicably in the kitchen. There was no sign of Quinn or Zach. That made her uneasy.

Becca looked up, her warm smile both charming and kind. Zach was a lucky man.

Maddie pulled out a chair and sat down, noting without being obvious about it, that one of her books lay on the table in front of Becca.

Becca noticed, of course. She and her siblings were learning that Becca was no slouch in the brains department.

"One of my favorite authors," she said, with a grin. "But that name." She shook her head.

"Yeah, in hindsight that was a mistake," Maddie admitted. She glanced around, casually, she hoped. "Where are the guys?"

"Taking a walk," Becca said, her lips twitching.

Maddie bit back the words she would have said if Gammie weren't there.

"I could have told him my Quinnie is fine," Gammie said, "but men. They always have to find out themselves."

"I hope Zach isn't giving him *the talk*," Maddie said, the words slipping out after all. She'd heard about the talk from her siblings, had seen a couple of them with her own eyes. They were beyond embarrassing. "We've known each other for two days."

"Zach was always a fan of *Perry Mason*," Becca said, instead of responding to Maddie's words. "He's consoling himself with that."

It was true that Perry had solved crimes. If Maddie had to be a lawyer, the least she could do was solve crimes.

"I don't solve crimes, at least not really." Her books were based on real events with lots of fiction mixed in. "I make up a lot of stuff."

"It is an interesting line you walk," Becca agreed.

"This one of your books?" Gammie asked, grabbing it off the table. At Maddie's nod she opened it and glanced down. "Need my glasses to see that."

If it was an excuse, it was a valid one. Maddie bit back a grin when the old lady put the book back down on the table. She patted it as if to make up for the rejection.

"It's thick."

"I made up a lot of stuff," Maddie said, once she got her twitching lips back under control. "The thing is," she went on, "no one takes them seriously. I mean, as far as I know, no one has gone to jail or anything."

"But the killers were already dead," Becca pointed.

Maybe she had read the books. Or she could do math on how many years old the crimes were from reading the blurbs. But based on what she knew of Becca, she'd read them. And long before she knew Maddie had written them.

"I was kind of running out of old cases to write about. It's tricky when some of the people involved are still alive."

That earned Maddie an arched brow from Gammie.

"Should I apologize? Or die so you can solve my murder?"

Maddie got a discreetly sympathetic look from Becca.

"It's a legal issue," Maddie said. "If I name a killer who is still alive, I can get sued."

"But you're doing it," Becca said, making it almost a question.

"Kind of." She was currently tiptoeing into uncharted territory with the book in progress.

"Couldn't you just change the names? Wouldn't that be enough?" Becca asked it outright this time.

"No. But people don't mind talking about their murder—" Maddie shot a look at Gammie, "if they didn't do it."

"Is it likely the authorities would reopen the case based on something you bring up in a book?" Becca looked thoughtful, as if she were trying to think through the ramifications Maddie might face.

"I can't begin to answer that," Maddie said. "The only cop currently interested in me right now is the one looking into the death of Quinn's neighbor."

Gammie perked up. "Quinnie's neighbor was killed?"

Maddie blinked. It was hard to keep track of the various threads coming at her from all directions.

"That's why Quinn came to see me," Maddie tried to explain. "I kind of used his neighbor's name as my pen name. And now he's dead." Saying the words out loud made her give an inner flinch. Was it her fault he was dead?

Before the guilt could build too far, the back door opened, and the men returned. Zach came in first, his cop walk more pronounced. Most of the time the walk was natural, a part of who he was and who he'd been. But age had taken its toll. She had noticed that when trouble threatened, putting his cop instincts on high alert, his cop walk came back with a vengeance.

Quinn looked impassive, but his gaze met hers for a fleeting moment, filled with wry amusement. It seemed to indicate the *talk* had happened and that he'd never had it before. This idea pleased her for reasons she didn't want to examine in her dad's presence.

Both men sat down, their elbows coming to rest on the table-top. Maddie leaned forward, resting hers there, too. After a pause, so did Becca.

It was kind of funny. Gammie shot them a look but then apparently decided the breach of etiquette didn't matter at the moment since no one was eating. At least, that's what Maddie decided.

Her sleep last night had been periods of deep, dream ladened chunks she jerked out of, then fell back into. There seemed to be pieces of all the problems, all the crimes, but weirdly distorted.

The end result, she'd woken without feeling much rested. And she still had to figure out what to do about the cop and the others. It was probably a bad idea to avoid the cop, but she couldn't figure out what he wanted.

"It's all a bit of a mess, isn't it?" Zach said finally, breaking the silence.

Maddie had figured that out by herself, but she knew better than to say it. She also knew her dad well enough to know there was an implication that this all could have been avoided if she'd been honest with him in the first place.

"Yes." Maddie had asked for it, so she admitted it. "It is a mess."

"The problem," Zach went on as if she hadn't spoken, "is the pieces that don't fit."

She knew this, too, but he was bringing different "eyes on" to the problem, so she tipped her head. "Like?"

"Like all of them. None of the murders were contiguous. Different times, different places, different people. Murders yes, but the crimes that prompted them were different, too. On the surface, you are the only connecting link."

Zach didn't like that, this was obvious.

"Yes," Maddie said doubtfully, "but also no. There's no way any of them could know I might write a book about their murder. The only person who knew..."

She stopped. Helen. Her editor. Who, as far as Maddie could tell from her research, had no link to any of the murders either.

"Who?" Zach perked up.

"My editor." Maddie met his narrowed gaze. "Who lives in New York. And who has been in possession of the information on *possible* upcoming book ideas for about three years."

Everyone was quiet, their eyes indicating processing was happening on a variety of levels. Zach finally sighed.

"If she was the only person who had this information, then you have assume she is the source of the leak, or whatever you'd call it," Zach said in his best cop voice.

Maddie had just come to that conclusion herself, but... "Wouldn't she have said something about it or tried to steer me away from one of them. She's had plenty of time."

Would it have worked if she'd tried? Maybe, Maddie thought, but there'd been a kind of hierarchy to her list. She was currently working—or trying to work—on the first murder on that list and Helen knew that. And Gammie's murder had been last and the least likely because of how sparse the information available was.

What had caught her attention, Maddie wondered now. It was an old, obscure murder, only made slightly interesting by the hint of scandal surrounding it. And the lack of justice.

All unsolved murders were defined by a lack of justice, but the ones that caught her eye felt more unjust, if that made sense. She must be more like Zach than she realized, she thought a bit wryly.

But there was also another factor to that list. Helen had wanted to know Maddie could deliver more books and she'd been filling in blanks. And Gammie's murder was the only "local" unsolved murder that she'd found that day.

So, it had actually been a mixture of justice and desperation —with a touch of gut instinct. And she'd also known that Helen wouldn't hold her to that list if she found something more interesting.

She looked up and found Gammie watching her.

"What made you reach out to me now?" Maddie asked. Quinn's reason made a little sense, but Gammie?

Gammie lifted her chin. "I saw an article about the author dying, the one it said wrote the books. It said he looked into unsolved murders, and I mentioned it to my neighbor, Ruth. You remember Ruth, Quinnie?"

Quinn shifted in his seat as both Zach and Becca looked at him.

"Of course. She's got the corner house where she can keep track of everything happening in the neighborhood."

"That's the one. I told her it was a pity because maybe he'd have tackled our murder. Well, she told me it wasn't the author who had died and I should get a hold of him." She paused to give Maddie a severe look. "It wasn't that easy. But Ruth's daughter's niece on her husband's side is better than Ruth about finding things out and she got me the information. Then Henry, her brother's son's wife's nephew gave me a lift. I don't think you've met him, Quinnie. He drives one of those big trucks. I had such a time getting up in it and getting out of it."

"He drove a big truck into..." Maddie said the words faintly. Surely the big truck hadn't driven into this neighborhood?

"Of course not, girl. He had a friend who drove one of those Uber things."

It was Quinn who brought the conversation back to an essential truth. "And while you were gone, someone planted a bomb in the old office."

And Ruth, the nosy and helpful neighbor, would have started spreading the news as soon as Gammie was hoisted up into that big truck.

"It was a pretty sophisticated device," Quinn went on.

"Everyone is sophisticated with the help of AI," Maddie said dryly. She used Chat and Grok for research. "They aren't supposed to, of course," she added when it looked like Quinn would object, "but there are workarounds for pretty much everything."

"I never go into that office," Gammie objected. She gazed off to the side. "Not since..."

"But if you saw the door ajar?" Quinn put in.

"I'd close it." Gammie's lips firmed into a straight line that added more wrinkles to her parchment skin. "Anyone that knows me knows that. And I don't know why anyone would bother. I've got one foot in the grave and the other hanging over it."

"And anyone who knows you," Quinn said, "knows you're too stubborn to die when you've got the bull by the horns. You want this murder solved."

To clear Walter. Her husband.

"It's more likely they'd have hurt someone other than me," Gammie said tartly, clearly annoyed. "My cleaner. The yard man. The meter reader. Even the mailman might have noticed."

"Would they have looked in?" Quinn pressed.

Gammie shrugged. "People are nosy. The fact that it's been locked all these years?"

Yeah, Maddie sighed. It was probably a local legend.

"Does that mean we think it's your murder causing all this?" Maddie couldn't help but feel doubtful. The timeline? What was the timeline? Quinn's Fitz-D had been dead for two days before she saw the news, started getting calls. But, unless Gammie was fudging events or she'd been talking about "her" murder for a long time, that connection had to be within the last twenty-four hours.

Zach frowned and gave a half shrug.

"There are those other two calls you had, Maddie," Quinn said.

She didn't need the reminder. She'd been thinking about them, too.

"They do appear to be related to two other cases on my list," Maddie said.

"Glad to hear you starting to have some skepticism," Zach said.

It was Maddie's turn to give him a look.

"Anyone raised by you wouldn't dare to be anything else," she pointed out. "And I'm plenty skeptical about all of it. Because it doesn't make any sense.'

"Murder," Zach said, "never does. Not really. There's logic in it, of course, if you can find it, but the act of it puts the murderer outside common sense and the normal."

"And all of the murders," Becca said, thoughtfully, "are old. Except for one."

"Sol. My neighbor." Quinn gave a heavy sigh.

"And the attempted one on Gammie," Maddie said.

Gammie madę a humphing sound. "Pretty sad attempt."

It hadn't felt sad at the time, Maddie thought. She still had a nice bruise on the shoulder that had impacted with the ground. She pushed that aside.

"If you were investigating this case, Zach," Maddie asked, "how would you go about it?"

Zach might have looked a bit offended. He might have intended to point out that he was at the least, helping with the case, but Becca put a hand on his and patted it.

Wow, Becca had superpowers, Maddie thought. Not that she thought that would work for her.

"I'd start with the murder in front of me," Zach said.

"Would you leave Plonkville and drive up here to talk to me?" Maddie asked. That seemed so odd, but she wasn't a cop.

Zach took the question seriously, judging by the deep crease between his brows. "All he has is the name, right?"

"That's all I know of," Maddie said, glancing at Quinn. He'd had a name and his gut instinct. So, it was possible Cop Plonkville was following his gut, too. Had he ever told her his name?

"I might," Zach said finally, "though he'd have to make the case to his chief to do it." He looked at Quinn. "You sure there's nothing in his life or past that could be suspicious?"

"I can't guarantee it," Quinn admitted. "But whoever killed him tossed his place." He gave a half shrug. "No way for me to know if they found what they were looking for. I've been in his place a couple of times and the usual things someone would steal were still there. TV. Computer."

"Tough case for a cop," Zach muttered. "Yeah, I'd follow the name path."

Maddie heaved a bigger sigh than her last. Great.

"It's going to get out, isn't it?"

No one asked what she meant. "I should probably call Helen. My editor," she added. "She should hear it from me."

Zach frowned. "Are you sure that's wise?"

"I wish we could keep it on the down-low until we know what's going on," Quinn agreed. "If this about you as author, the longer we keep that quiet the better."

Zach actually gave him an approving look. "I agree."

"It might explain why no one has tried to injure Maddie," Becca said, her eyes reflecting worry now. "I mean, so far it appears they are trying to find the author through you?"

Even as her own agent, she didn't see how this could end well if someone was trying to get to her as the author. Witnesses, she knew from long experience, were inconvenient to murderers.

"Well," Maddie spoke into the silence that had fallen after Becca's words, "I probably should call Cop Plonkville. Since he is a cop."

Quinn glanced at Zach and saw what he'd expected. Zach was conflicted about that, too. The cop in him thought it was the right thing to do. The dad? Not so much.

"Do we know he is your cop from Plonkville?" Quinn asked. It was a small police department. He'd met one guy after he reported Sol's death. His lips thinned at that memory. He'd been young, eager and then suddenly sobered by what had probably been his first murder. "I know they had to bring in the Parish crime scene techs to process the scene."

Maddie looked thoughtful. "I wouldn't know. I only spoke to him on the phone." She looked at him with a trace of a smile. "I can't believe you live in a place called Plonkville."

He chuckled, welcoming the slight easing of tension.

"Neither can I," Gammie said, an edge to her voice.

He wished Maddie hadn't brought it up. It was an old sore point between him and Gammie, but he'd needed the space from all of his family after he'd been pushed out of the SEALS. Gammie had been sure he'd become a suicide statistic without her watching eye. He hadn't argued the point. The statistics didn't lie.

He was pretty sure Sol had been worried, too. Quinn, as far as he could tell, had been the only person the old hermit had allowed through the door. And that would be why he had to find out who killed him and why. That his determination had brought him into contact with Maddie might be a positive. The thought of her twelve siblings and her old man was daunting, no question.

But he'd faced down terrorists. He should be fine. He felt his lips twitch, looked up and caught Zach looking at him as if he'd known exactly what Quinn had been thinking.

That sobered him up.

"Let's bring your cop here," Zach said grimly, his attention and gaze turning back to Maddie. "I'll know if he's the real deal."

"And if he isn't?" Maddie protested. "I'll bring him here. Into your lives." She gave a pointed look at Becca.

It was obvious Zach didn't like that train of thought.

"I should meet him at the office," Maddie said. "He already knows about it and Gideon and Frank can take care of themselves."

"I don't like it," Quinn said at the same time as Zach.

"We could have Alex arrange a meeting at the station," Zach said.

Quinn saw Maddie roll her eyes. "You want to bake him, don't you?"

Zach shrugged and the grin he gave was smug. "I do. Even if he's the real deal, he needs to know who he's dealing with."

Maddie's brows arched. "An honest citizen?"

"Sure," Zach agreed. He studied Maddie for several seconds. "What's the problem, Baby?"

Maddie's lips thinned and she looked away.

"I think," Becca said, "that Maddie is perfectly capable of handling herself in this, or any situation. She is, after all, a Baker."

Baby. Quinn felt the light dawn. She was the youngest.

"She came to you for advice, now perhaps you should give her some space to decide how she wants to handle things."

Quinn noticed Becca had put her hand over Zach's clenched one on the tabletop.

"Thank you, Becca."

Maddie's sudden, brilliant smile almost dazzled Quinn. His breath caught and his heart clenched painfully.

"Would it be alright if I helped?" he asked, surprised he managed to get the words out.

Maddie turned to him, the smile still in place.

"You may," she said.

He didn't know he'd smiled back until her dad humphed again.

10

Maddie had missed one whole day at the office, but it felt as if it hadn't been dusted or cleaned in a month. Not that she cleaned it on the days she was there. She did like to spray some stuff around to remove, however briefly, the damp that inhabited every enclosed space in New Orleans.

She also felt weirdly bereft about leaving her laptop with Becca. She'd done what work she could, and she and Quinn had studied the security video of all three of her possible "clients."

Quinn didn't recognize the cop. The other two—one man, one woman—both wore hats. His was of the gimme variety and hers would have looked better on the beach. But the hats shadowed their faces. Did that mean they knew about the security camera?

Quinn wouldn't commit either way because their clothes didn't clash with their hats. Maddie couldn't disagree with him on that one, though the woman's hat was more obviously matched to her sundress.

Which was the Darrow and which was the Merrick, she wondered. And was the cop a cop? It felt a bit like a Laurel and Hardy "Who's on first" skit but with all the humor removed.

Without her computer, she wasn't sure what to do. Both Frank and Gideon weren't in yet, so Quinn snagged a chair from Frank's office. It wouldn't fit in her space, so he positioned it in the open doorway and settled himself on it with his arms crossed over his chest.

"You okay?" he asked, without looking at her.

"I'm not great," she said. "Without my laptop, I mean. I usually use this kind of time to work on my book." She didn't know what to do with her hands and she shifted restlessly in her chair. "We don't even know if they'll come back."

The words had barely left her mouth when they heard footsteps out in the hallway. Maddie sat up straighter. Quinn didn't move.

The handle rattled, and then the door eased open and a woman peered in. A woman with a big sun hat. She'd changed to a different sundress though.

"Come in," Maddie said, resisting the impulse to say they didn't bite. She didn't but she wasn't sure what Quinn might do if things got dicey.

The woman moved awkwardly, like a colt not yet sure of its footing. Only she wasn't young. She was in that indeterminate place between the fifties and sixties, Maddie decided. It was, according to Becca, when women became almost invisible. Maybe the sun hat was her answer to that.

Maddie rose. Normally she could look at people over her laptop. Only she didn't have it. Her Della Street vibe was seriously off balance. Quinn had risen to his feet at the sight of the woman. He did have nice manners.

"How can I help you?"

"I was here yesterday," the woman said. "Mr. Baker…"

She faltered to a stop.

If it weren't for the sun hat, Maddie might have wondered if she were here to see one of her brothers.

"This was a mistake," the woman finally said. "I don't know why I came."

Maddie stepped around her desk and indicated her chair. "Why don't you sit down."

After a wary glance at Quinn, the woman eased past her and sank into the chair as if she were exhausted.

Maddie exchanged a glance with Quinn. He gave a slight shrug.

"My brother said you'd stopped by."

"Your brother?" The woman looked up sharply. And then nodded. "Of course. Your brother. Baker. Baker."

Candlestick maker. Maddie didn't say it out loud. And it wasn't quite right anyway. She gave herself a mental shake.

"He couldn't read his handwriting." Maddie infused some humor into her voice. "You are..."

The woman hesitated. "Darrow. Mildred Darrow."

Maddie realized she had a handbag clutched to her chest.

"This is embarrassing. I'm not sure why...how." She took a steadying breath and looked up. "I got this letter, you see."

"A letter?" Maddie exchanged a puzzled look with Quinn.

She opened her bag and extracted a sheet, hesitated, and then held it out to Maddie.

Maddie took it, unfolded it, and read.

S.C. Fitz-Dankworthington is writing a book about the Darrow murder. He will find the truth and it won't set you free.

A friend.

The letter was typed, like seriously typed on an actual type-writer. She held it out for Quinn to read.

"How did you know to come here?"

"It was a voicemail. Weird voice. It gave me your name, at least, M. Baker?"

Maddie nodded.

"And this address."

"Interesting," Maddie murmured. And not in a good way interesting.

"At first, I didn't, I wasn't, but then I started to worry. I was young when it happened, you see, just a kid really, but I remember everyone being upset." A pale sort of smile edged her mouth. "I might have been kind of excited by the drama of it all."

She twisted the soft handle of her bag between her fingers.

"That seems pretty normal. Kids are ghouls." At least she and her siblings had been.

"Yes, I suppose." She paused and then continued, "As I grew up, I realized, or became aware of the damage." She looked up beseechingly. "It's over or at least in the past. Couldn't you talk to him and explain. We don't, we just...I just want to live my life."

It was a point of view she should have thought of, she thought. Not everyone wanted the truth and that didn't make them guilty, just human.

"He wasn't necessarily planning to write about the Darrow case," Maddie told her. "But I will talk to...him." It was harder to keep the lie going, but Zach was right. Now was not the time to out herself.

Mildred looked relieved, as if she saw something reassuring in Maddie's face. She rose, holding out her hand.

Maddie shook it. "He's not trying to upset people's lives. For him it's just a puzzle to be solved," she tried to explain.

"I like puzzles," Mildred said, looking interested in the idea. "I guess if I didn't know—I'd be intrigued, too. Thank you for your time."

Quinn held the door for her, and they didn't speak as they listened to her footsteps retreating down the hallway.

Maddie propped her hip on the edge of her desk, too restless to sit down again. "Do you suppose our Mr. Merrick got a letter, too?"

"Seems likely," Quinn said. "And now I'm wondering if Gam —my grandmother got one, too?"

Maddie hadn't followed her thoughts that far yet, but it made sense.

"Why wouldn't she tell you?"

"I don't know why she does what she does." Quinn said it with an edge of sourness. Then gave her a wry grin. "She's an original. I don't know how they manage it here, but it seems like all the grandmas are originals."

Maddie chuckled. "I never knew my grandparents. I have a great aunt." But she didn't know her that well. That story was too complicated to add into her brain processes at the moment. And when she did think about it, it made her eye twitch.

Whatever Quinn might have planned to say or ask, he was stopped by the sound of more footsteps. These were different, probably male. Mr. Merrick or the cop?

It was the gimme cap. His story was essentially the same, though delivered with more annoyance and a few threats of legal action. Maddie gave him the same promise to talk to "that author fella stirring up trouble." He didn't appear appeased, but he must have realized he couldn't actually do anything about a book that hadn't been written.

Quinn's presence put a damper on him, too, and he finally took himself off, a bit more stamp to his footsteps as he retreated.

"All that's left is the cop," Maddie said.

"And we know something important," Quinn said.

Maddie looked at him with a lifted brow.

"We know your list was definitely leaked to someone, to someone who doesn't want the truth to get out."

Maddie nodded. "But we still don't know which one." All

three of them had a plausible story, including Quinn's Gammie. And including Quinn.

And she looked at that thought with an effort at dispassion? His was the thinnest of them all. She stared at the wooden door and wondered just how good her instincts were.

QUINN WOULD HAVE LIKED to get up and pace, but there wasn't room.

"You know you probably need to talk to your editor."

Maddie nodded, still without looking at him. Was she realizing just how thin all their stories were? Including his? She'd trusted him further than he'd had a right to expect. He should give her distance. That's what her dad had said to him last night. But how could he leave her here alone?

Her brother had been here when someone had tried to lift her laptop. Okay, maybe tried to lift it. But the bathroom? And the incident in the cafe? Too many coincidences.

Maddie sighed. "I know." Now she did look at him, her gaze wry and amused. "I can write all kinds of words in a book, most of them totally made up, and I don't know what to say to her. I can't even imagine that conversation."

"You're sure she's the only one..."

"I'm sure." Maddie's tone was definite. "I mean, she's had it for two years, so she probably didn't leak it or anything. Someone in her office could have seen it. It's not like it's some state secret or anything."

"She would have wanted to keep it confidential, though, right? So no one else stole the idea?"

"Stole the idea?" Maddie frowned, clearly considering this. "Even if someone took it and wrote their version...I mean, I guess she might worry about that."

"You wouldn't mind?" He pressed.

"Seriously? No. How I would write the story wouldn't be like anyone else, even if we came to the same conclusion. There aren't actually any original ideas, just unique ways of looking at the same thing."

A small silence fell. She looked at her watch.

"I wish I knew if the cop was late or not coming back."

"Yeah," Quinn agreed. He hadn't recognized the guy in the security footage, but that didn't mean he wasn't Plonkville PD or even a parish deputy working the case. He wanted to suggest getting a snack or something, but that hadn't gone so well last time. It was his turn to sigh. "I know there's nothing I can say to reassure you that I'm not in this, whatever it is."

She shifted to more fully face him. "No, probably not." She appeared to think, then grinned. "Nope, can't think of anything."

In spite of himself, he laughed.

"I..." he began, then stopped.

Footsteps. Again.

Maddie retreated back behind the desk, taking her seat once again, her hands clasped on the desktop. Quinn didn't sit down. He felt coiled for trouble, following an instinct he couldn't have explained if his life depended on it. He wished Maddie had gone into the other office.

The door opened without the hesitation of the two previous visitors. But then it would.

It was Gideon. He looked at them both in surprise. "You're here."

"Yes," Maddie said.

"I ran into that cop downstairs and told him I didn't think you were."

"Oh." Maddie looked at him.

Gideon frowned. "What's going on, Mads?"

"I'll have to get back to you on that one," Maddie said, rising with a calm that Quinn was pretty sure she didn't feel. "I probably won't be in for a few days."

Gideon's frown deepened. "Why not?"

"I think I'm going to go to Plonkville," she said.

Gideon looked at him and he shrugged. "Plonkville," he echoed. She must be following her gut because he couldn't think of any reason to go there.

"Zach should have spanked you more," Gideon said, standing back so they could leave.

Maddie looked back over her shoulder. "By the time I was born, he was too tired."

Quinn heard Gideon laughing as they left.

11

Plonkville, Maddie decided, was movie, or perhaps TV show, cute. It had quaint houses, tree-lined streets—the trees artistically draped with moss—and an air of serenity in the quiet afternoon. It could have made it into any Hallmark movie. Or, if one liked contrast, a horror movie. Maddie could totally visualize zombies coming around the corner, but she wasn't surprised when it was just a battered pickup truck advertising someone's plumbing business on the side.

"You picked it because of the name, didn't you?"

Quinn grinned, not taking his eyes off the road. "Of course. Drives my family around the bend every time they have to say it."

See, her instincts had been right on about him. She loved a sense of humor edged with a little dark. She'd learned "tweaking siblings" from an early age. Could probably be awarded a master's degree in it.

So far, her siblings had chosen partners that could take the heat in or out of the kitchen. Not that she wanted to bring Quinn into that kitchen. But if she did, he could hold his own, she was sure.

They turned down what seemed to be the main drag, Maddie decided, based on the quaint stores on either side. The street fed into a small square with a courthouse holding pride of place.

Maddie noticed a uniformed man mounting the steps and pointed him out and the truck slowed.

"I think that's the guy who responded to my call," Quinn said.

It wasn't the guy in the video, which made her uneasy. Plonkville didn't have a big force, just the two, she thought recalled.

Quinn found a place to park and helped Maddie down to the street. The still air held the faint hint of something sweet that was either baking or had been. She searched the square and found the small bakery tucked in between an antique shop and a bookstore. It was probably ironic that a copy of her book was positioned in the window of the bookstore.

Not my book, she reminded herself, *at least don't think of that now. It's Fitz-D's.*

She lagged a little behind Quinn who had called out to the police officer, her thoughts drifting off into wondering what would change in her life when it got out that she was the author? Did she want it to get out? She wasn't sure. It was something she should probably figure out. She didn't want to. She wanted to figure out how to write the last third of her book.

She looked up and realized she was far enough behind to have an excellent view of Quinn's back. Broad shoulders nicely hugged by his tee shirt. And well, his jeans had to be pleased with their fit.

She met the police officer's gaze and smiled, hoping he was too far away to see the heat in her cheeks.

They both turned as she joined them.

"This is M. Baker," Quinn said, taking her elbow to pull her closer.

Maddie watched the officer and saw no reaction to her name. Quinn's grip tightened briefly, then relaxed.

"Any updates on Sol's murder?"

"The Parish guys took it over."

The police officer looked a bit glum.

"Do you know who's in charge?"

The officer frowned.

"He was my neighbor," Quinn said. "I found the body."

"Oh right."

The office pulled out his phone and unlocked it. After a minute, he gave Quinn the contact information.

Then they were alone again, Quinn showed her the number. It wasn't the same as the one she'd received from the so-called cop.

Quinn looked around, located a bench and directed her toward it. They sat in silence for several minutes.

"It could have been a different detective who called you," Quinn said finally.

There was really only one way to find out. She needed to call him. She didn't want to. She wanted to go check out that bakery. She was a connoisseur of bakeries. She should write a book about bakeries she'd known and loved.

"Maddie?"

Quinn's voice was low and the hand that covered hers warmed her. She hadn't known she was cold. Interesting. She looked down at their hands and shivered. It was cooler in the shade.

"Do think I'm really in trouble?" The question surprised her. She looked up at him. She'd surprised Quinn, too.

"You have doubts?"

"Not doubts exactly. It just all feels...unreal." That was the right word for it. Unreal. "I feel like I'm living in one of my books. No," she flashed him a wry grin, "not one of mine. I'm not this fictional."

Quinn gave a small chuckle. "Truth being stranger than fiction?"

"Apparently." She repressed a longing to lean against him. And then he lifted his arm and looped it around her shoulders. It felt so right. She let herself relax a little into his hold, soaking up comfort and something more from the contact.

His hold tightened and he said, his voice rough, "Maddie..."

"Mr. Ellery?"

The voice broke snapped the thread that had been forming between them. She looked up, squinting at the figure blocking the light. She lifted her hand to shade her eyes.

He definitely looked like a cop in the way he held himself. She also knew he wasn't the man they'd seen in the security video and his voice didn't match the voice of whoever had called her. Did three strikes make her out?

"I'm Robbie G. Lee, lead investigator for the Fitz-Dankworthington murder. Young Bubba says you wanna talk to me."

Quinn rose and shook the man's hand. "This is Ms. Baker."

Robbie G. Lee didn't react to her name at all.

Maddie shook hands, too, got a once over that felt more like a guy looking at a gal, than a cop looking at a suspect.

"What can I help you with?" Robbie G. Lee hooked his thumbs in his belt, the movement giving her a glimpse of his handgun in a shoulder holster.

"I was the one who found Sol."

"That's right."

"I was wondering if there'd been any progress made?"

Robbie G. Lee studied him for several long seconds. "How well did you know the victim?"

Quinn shrugged. "We were neighbors for two years. He wasn't...he didn't."

"According to the other neighbors he was a hermit, grouchy, standoffish...did I miss anything?"

Quinn made a wry face. "I don't think so. He was an ornery old man. Did you know he was Special Forces?"

"Was he now?" Robbie G. Lee's expression was considering. "Did you know that no one of that name was in any military force?"

Quinn frowned. "I couldn't be wrong. He..."

"I said *no one by that name*," Robbie G. Lee interrupted him.

"His name wasn't..." Maddie's interjection wasn't planned. "He made it up?"

"From a whole cloth. Looks like he did it about ten years ago."

He made it up. Maddie wanted to laugh. He made up his name and she made up an author using that name. If that wasn't irony, she didn't know what was.

Quinn sank back down on his bench. He rubbed his face. "I liked him. He had the right moves, he knew his stuff." He looked up and must have seen something in Robbie G. Lee's face because he went on, "I was a Navy SEAL. You learn to recognize..."

Robbie G. Lee pursed his lips and nodded. "That might be helpful in figuring out who he really was. Narrow the search a bit. Amazing what you can find out with this artificial intelligence and facial recognition techno stuff. Special Forces. That should help, too."

His tone was slightly disparaging and slightly admiring. As if he wanted to stand up for good old-fashioned detecting and couldn't.

She turned her attention toward a random drift of donut smell and tried not to sigh. She always thought better after a donut or two. She really needed to get past wondering if—or how—any of this connected to her or her books. She couldn't dismiss any of it. The phone calls, the letters, the weird attempts on her...laptop?

In fiction, amateur sleuths got into trouble because they withheld information from the proper authorities. If this were a novel, she'd think she was smarter than the cop and better equipped to take on the killer than the armed officer.

But as the daughter of a cop, the sister of a variety of law enforcement siblings, she knew she wasn't smarter than Robbie G. Lee. And his gun looked bigger than hers.

No, the problem wasn't the idea of sharing. It was what kind of information she had on offer. No one liked to look stupid or crazy. She had a series of weird, possibly random events that so far added up to...crazy.

She came back to the moment and realized Robbie G. Lee was regarding her with an interest that was clearly professional.

Zach had taken her seriously, or had pretended he had? Or he was her dad, so he was going to worry even if he thought it was random and crazy, too.

"Did you have something you want to tell me?" Robbie G. Lee said.

"I don't," Maddie said frankly, "but I probably should. You don't lock people up for sounding crazy anymore, do you?"

"Only the dangerously crazy ones." Robbie G. Lee looked amused. "Why don't you sit yourself down next to Mr. Quinn here and tell me what's on your mind?"

His tone was lazy, as if he didn't have anything else to do. Maddie was impressed by that. She wondered how fast that would change.

"My name is M. Baker. Maddie, but I use M for my business." Again, no reaction from Robbie G. Lee. "At least, I use M. Baker

as a literary lawyer. One of my clients is S.C. Fitz-Dankworthington."

That sent Robbie G. Lee's eyes brows up. Then he frowned.
"Did I read something about that?"

"Some people initially thought your victim was my author,
but it died down quickly because it wasn't true." Maddie hesitated again, but Robbie G. Lee didn't say anything. "Someone
from here, from the Plonkville Police Department called me a
couple of days ago about it. It was the first I'd heard of it myself."

What was she tiptoeing through? A minefield or cartoon
daisies?

Robbie G. Lee frowned again. "That wasn't in the report they
passed on. Which officer was it that called you?"

Maddie shrugged. "Looking back, I'm not sure if he gave me
his name." She extracted her phone, found the unknown
number in recents, and showed it to him.

He took out his own phone and made a note of the number.
"Have you tried calling it?"

Maddie hesitated, glancing at Quinn. "I haven't. Some odd
things have happened, and well my author and your victim
couldn't be related."

"And yet here you are with him." Robbie G. Lee nodded
toward Quinn.

"I looked her up," Quinn said. "I thought it was an odd coincidence that Sol and her author had almost the same name." He
met the detective's gaze squarely. "It was something to do."

Robbie G. Lee nodded as if he understood. "He was your
friend."

"Well, I'm not sure he'd have said that, but yeah. I liked the
old geezer. And," his hands curled into fists, "someone killed
him. I don't like that."

"I don't either," Robbie G. Lee said, almost soothingly. "And

I'd like to find who did it. I'm still not sure where you come in, ma'am."

His turn back to her startled Maddie.

"I'm not sure either." She looked up, making a helpless gesture with her hands. "This is the part where I start to sound crazy."

She started at the beginning and told him almost all of it, omitting only the part where she was the author. To his credit, Robbie G. Lee listened to her without interrupting and he even took the occasional note. When she fell silent, he didn't speak immediately, and she felt that he was considering all she had told him. Maybe looking for a way to pat her on the head and send her on her way.

Finally, he his chest heaved as he took a deep breath. "That is a very curious story, ma'am." He rubbed a hand across the bristle of his hair. "To tell you the truth, if I had a slightly decent lead, I'd already be driving away to check it out."

He paced away from them. Stopped. Turned around and paced back. "Since I'm already spinning my wheels, I might as well waste my time checking out your story. Let me have the names of the people involved. And I'll need your security footage."

"I uploaded it to my phone," Maddie said, diffidently. She wasn't sure if she was relieved, he was going to check things out, when it seemed evident that he didn't quite believe her. It didn't feel like a win. More like a draw.

She air-dropped him the footage and then watched him study it. He finally shook his head. "I don't recognize the officer. That doesn't mean he isn't one," he added, as if afraid she'd get uppity or something.

Robbie G. Lee headed back toward the courthouse, possibly to start the inquiries process.

"I notice you've been side eyeing that donut shop," Quinn said. "Shall we check it out?"

"Please," Maddie said, in her most heartfelt tone. "It might save my life, or at least my mind. It just keeps spinning and spinning."

They picked out donuts, with cold drinks to go with, and then returned to the square and their bench. It wasn't totally quiet. There were people, pets, cars, but the vibe was low key and slower moving than the city.

Maddie closed her eyes and stretched her legs out in front, nibbling slowly on the crisp—just the right amount of sweet—treat. She finished one, licked her lips and then tipped the cold soft drink up for a long swallow. She lowered the can, opened her eyes, but stared straight ahead as a small gaggle of school-girls in uniforms made their way across the square opposite them.

"How weird is it that your Sol and my," she hesitated. They appeared to be alone, but it was better not to talk about her secret in public. "My author both had made-up names?"

"Well, you...he picked that name because it was odd."

"Kind of the same reason you picked Plonkville," Maddie said.

"Exactly." He wiped his fingers with a napkin. "Sol's murder is the only solid thing we have. He died. And now we know he was hiding from something. Or someone."

"This could all be about his secret." Did she want to grab onto the idea because it made more sense than anything so far? Or because she just wanted it all to go away? She cast Quinn a sidelong glance. Except for him. He could stay.

～

WAS SHE STILL IN TROUBLE? Quinn tried to think his way through the situation, but as everyone involved had previously noted, it was a snarl, a quagmire of odd. All he could latch onto was his gut instinct, the same instinct that had taken him to New Orleans and his meeting with Maddie.

"I don't know," he finally said. He did know that the thought of walking away from her tightened his gut into nearly as many knots as the current situation.

"There's so much we don't know, that we can't know," she said, "so I've been thinking about what your..." a pause ... "your grandmother told us about her murder."

His lips twitched at this. His Gammie had become very proprietary about a murder she hadn't wanted to talk about for over sixty years. "Yes?" he prompted.

"Specifically, I've been thinking about James Carver, the missing husband." She stretched her legs out in front and crossed them. "I can only think of three reasons for him to have disappeared. He ran away because he was scared. He ran away because he killed Etta Mae. And..."

Her voice trailed off.

Quinn finished it for her. "He didn't run away because he's dead."

"If someone killed Etta Mae because of her marriage to a white man, they would surely have known which white man. Not that we know," Maddie murmured. "But it was probably easier to disappear him than Etta Mae. From what your grandmother said, he didn't have local ties. As far as she knew, no one came looking for him."

"If that's why Etta Mae was killed." Quinn said the words, even though he knew Gammie believed that was why she'd died. She hadn't said it, but it had been there in the story.

"Well, hopefully Robbie G. Lee will look into him a bit more."

Something in her tone had him shifting to look at her. "What?"

She gave him a mischievous look. "I just know someone who could probably find out."

"Someone?"

"My sister-in-law."

Quinn arched a brow.

"She's kind of epic. She hooked me up with these." She reached into her bag and pulled out a pair of sunglasses and held them out to him.

He took them, but reluctantly.

"Put them on."

Her lips twitched and what he wanted to do was kiss them. But he put them on. For a minute, he didn't realize... "Whoa." He turned his head one way, then the other, noting the rear view it gave him. "Takes a little getting used to."

"Yeah, it's all about your focus. It's harder when I'm walking, but this week was the first time I actually needed them."

"You weren't wearing them in the cafe," he said.

"In the cafe, I watched you."

Now it was his lips that twitched, mostly because he liked her words, liked the idea of her watching him.

"Your eyes," she added. "You were very cool, didn't give much away, but your eyes scanned and then they stopped and I knew.."

He held up the sunglasses. "I need to get me a pair of these."

"I'll ask Gemma if she can get you a dude version."

He chuckled and thought that something flickered in her eyes for a moment. She held up her phone.

"Do you think I should call her?"

He wanted to know, he realized. So, was he the right person to ask? "If we wait on the Robbie G," he said, "we will wait forever. He has no reason to update us on anything."

"True." She looked down at her phone, then unlocked it and dialed.

Usually, a person could hear a little of the other side of the conversation. Interesting that he couldn't hear a thing. He only knew the call had connected when she started to speak.

"Hey, Gemma, it's Maddie. How you doing? Still putting up with my brother?" She laughed. Listened for a bit, then got down to it. "I was wondering if you could do some of your special research for a client of mine? Nothing illegal, I promise." Another laugh. "Yes, I'm a lawyer, so doing something illegal would be bad." Another pause. "It's some names. Old names."

She then gave this Gemma the names Gammie had given them: James Carver and Leroy Washington. Also, their last known location.

"You're the best, thank you so much. I'll owe you some free legal advice or something." Maddie laughed again and the call apparently ended because she lowered her arm and phone.

"And now we wait?" Quinn asked, wondering what this Gemma could do that he or Maddie couldn't do with a computer and some time.

"I should probably head back to New Orleans," Maddie said, her tone reluctant and then, "I can see why you settled here. It's nice."

"You grew up in New Orleans, didn't you?" Could a city girl settle here? He'd been raised small town, so it hadn't been hard for him.

"I did." She glanced at him. "In a house with fourteen people vying for two bathrooms."

"I can't even imagine that," Quinn said. "I have two sisters and a brother." And his parents were both living still.

"What is it that you do?" Her brow creased. "I don't think you said? Other than being Sol's neighbor?"

He hadn't told her? That surprised him. He felt like they

already knew so much about each other. It was a strange sensation. "When I first mustered out, I didn't do much of anything. I hadn't had anything to spend my money on, so I looked around. Found this place. Bought a house. I guess you could call it consulting. I didn't want to become a mercenary, so I consult with people on self-protection." He cocked an eyebrow in her direction. "Sounds like your Gemma does it, too?"

"Gemma is an NCIS agent these days, but her previous job is a bit mysterious and vague. I'm pretty sure it was in a high-tech zone." She glanced up at him and grinned. "I just asked a random research question, not expecting an answer and she delivered in spades. I try not to bother her too often."

"A useful addition to your family," Quinn said. He needed better in-laws. One sold life insurance and the other real estate. Okay that sister-in-law had been useful when he bought his house.

"I feel a bit like an under achiever in all aspects," Maddie said with a sigh. "Alex married a children's book author, and his wife gave Zach his first grandchild. Cal's wife runs a catering business. I sometimes help her out at events for the free food. It's fabulous. Ben's significant other is a major creds geek. Zach isn't super thrilled with Eddie's girl. Her dad was an arsonist, but it does make her interesting. Gideon's wife came with a counterfeit classic car. It's pretty cool."

Quinn suppressed a laugh. "That is hard to keep up with."

She turned to give him a mock severe look. "Well, it is. I wasn't even doing criminal law."

This time he did laugh. "Maddie, if you were anymore interesting we'd probably both be dead."

Now she laughed with him and he realized he just might be in danger of falling in love. Someone had told him once, that love was the most high-risk mission of them all.

Was it an accident when they got up to stroll back to Quinn's truck that his fingers curled around hers? She hadn't held hands with a boy since high school. And her brothers had scared that boy off. She glanced at Quinn. He'd be hard to scare off if he wanted to stay. Did he? She was afraid to hope.

"How about we find somewhere to eat?" Quinn said, as he helped her up into the truck.

She almost joked about it being a date, but she managed to stop herself. "I'd like that," she said instead.

She was securing her seatbelt when she noticed Robbie G. Lee coming out onto the courthouse steps and looking around. Quinn had just climbed in behind the wheel.

"Quinn, look," she said. "Surely he's not looking for us."

"I'll find out." He was out and striding toward Robbie G. Lee almost before she could blink.

They spoke for a few minutes and then Quinn came back, his expression grim.

"What?" she asked as he rejoined her.

"They were digging foundations for a new subdivision not far from...my grandmother's house." He looked at her now. "They found a skeleton. A male. He talked to their cops about the information we provided, and it looks like they might be reopening the investigation into Etta Mae's death if it turns out to be Turner. They want us to head over there and talk to them."

Maddie blinked. Shouldn't it be Gammie they wanted to talk to?

"It's getting late," Maddie said. Yeah, she was curious, but she was also tired and wasn't sure where she'd be sleeping tonight.

Quinn looked at his watch and nodded his agreement. "I have a guest room." Did he think she would object? Because he added, "I don't like the idea of you being alone in a hotel."

Now that she thought about it, she didn't like that idea either. "That sounds good, if you're sure you don't mind."

She knew who would mind. Zach. But what he didn't know...

"Let's get some food first."

Quinn found a little place on a bayou with amazing seafood. Maddie didn't bring up their current problem and neither did Quinn. They talked about almost everything but that. It was dark when they turned on the little street where Quinn lived. It was easy to spot Sol's house. It still had crime scene tape on the door.

Quinn's house was a little frame cottage with a neat yard and painted fence. Trees from the yards on either side over hung enough to probably give him some nice shade. Inside was sparse but somehow not a surprise to Maddie.

Quinn showed her around with a matter-of-factness she appreciated. Dinner had felt like a date, not quite a first date, but not all the way to a second. She didn't want that level of comfort here. It was all too tempting. He was too tempting, and she didn't do tempting. She'd never seen the point.

The guest room was also sparse, but the bed looked comfortable, and she had her own bathroom. She turned to Quinn, stopped in the doorway, or rather on the other side of it.

"Anything you need?"

"It looks great, thanks," she said.

"Just holler if...." He stopped.

"If I see a bug, you know I will." She grinned and felt some of the tension dissipate.

He grinned in return. "Good night then, Maddie."

"Good night, Quinn."

12

It was hard to feel like they'd made any progress when Quinn steered his truck back towards Beauville. He'd slept lightly, much like when he'd been a SEAL and on alert. And yet, there'd been no sign of any opposition in Plonkville.

What would they find here? Had the bomb been a response to Gammie's murder talk? He didn't think there was anything else in her life that would provoke that response, but she'd lived a lot of her life before he'd arrived in the world. She could be a tough old biddy when she wanted to.

Maddie sat with her hands clasped in her lap. She'd gone quiet about five miles ago and he wondered what she was thinking.

His cellphone trilled, and on his truck's screen, the name and number popped up. *Gammie.*

He approved the call and her voice came out of the speakers.

"That you, Quinn?"

Quinn?

Something was wrong. His grip on the wheel tightened.

"Yeah. What's up?"

"I'm home and I need to talk to you. Are you where you can run over?"

Very un-Gammie-like.

He exchanged a look with Maddie and saw concern spiking in her gaze, too.

"Sure." He glanced at his watch. "I'm about an hour out." More like ten minutes, but he needed the time to think.

"I'll see you soon."

The call ended.

"So," Maddie said, "trouble?"

"Trouble."

"How," Maddie began and then stopped.

"What?"

"How did she end up at home? We left her with Zach and Becca. But it seems obvious someone tricked her into coming home."

"Yeah."

A road sign came up. They were eleven minutes out. There was time to loop in the local cops, but did he want to? Did he dare? Did he trust them? There was someone in the mix claiming to be a cop out there, but was he?

His mind raced. He knew how to get in and take down a threat, but without the tech and backup? And in broad daylight? Could he risk Gammie's life like that?

He glanced at Maddie again and caught her watching him. He realized she was giving him time and space to think, to plan.

"I have a gun," she said. "And I know how to use it."

"I don't want to kill anyone," he said.

"No, it could get awkward, but it is preferable to being murdered."

"True." He managed a grin though it was definitely wry. "Whoever it is, they are expecting me to walk in the door, all unsuspecting." And then what? Shoot or threaten? "She didn't mention you."

Was that from intent or orders from whoever was coercing her?

"I'm trying not to take that personally," Maddie said. Her grin wasn't wry at all, and it made his heart skip a beat.

He'd done a lot of dangerous things in his life, aware each time it might be his last. He didn't want today to be his last day. He wanted time to get to know this woman.

"Whoever is with Gammie," Maddie said, "they want more than to eliminate her as a witness. He, or possibly she, thinks we know something. Or thinks you know something. Otherwise, they'd just have killed her and moved on."

"It's possible. If it is about Etta Mae's murder," he conceded. But what else could it be about? It had to be that. Zach had said it. There were a lot of distractions, but in the end, you had to focus on the murder in front of your face. Or, in Gammie's case, attempted murder? Planned murder?

"Last night, they just thought the body might be Leroy's, right?"

Quinn nodded. "They were following the lead, probably because it was *a* lead."

"But there's been no definite ID that we know of yet, so whoever is holding Gammie, might not know that it's possibly too late. There are multiple people who know what we know or suspect."

"Yes," he agreed, wondering where her mind was going with this.

"Well, I think we just go in and see what's going on." She held up a hand as he opened his mouth. "I know, crazy. He could just shoot us both. But this person must know you used to be a SEAL. Won't he expect you to come in the back way or something?"

Her logic wasn't awful, though it went against his training and instincts. Were his instincts protesting? Or just his logic?

"There is no "we" here. I go in alone."

As if he hadn't spoken, she continued thoughtfully, "Or I could go in and you could rescue us both."

"Maddie..."

"Whoever it is thinks he has the upper hand. But he's alone with Gammie. And you're a SEAL and I'm just some lawyer who happens to be concealed carrying. Surely, we can do something with that?"

"Gammie," Quinn found it hard to get the words out, "might already be dead."

"Yes." Maddie's tone was even. "We could drive straight to the police station."

"That's what we probably should do."

"Zach would vote for that option."

"I could drop you at the police station and go in myself while you bring help."

Her hand suddenly clutched his arm, not enough to disrupt his driving, but as if she wanted to hold on to him.

"I can do that, if that's what you want. She's your grandmother."

And Gammie probably didn't want him to just walk in. He knew she'd say, she was old. But she was his grandmother, his Gammie.

"Let's split the difference," he said, finally. "I'll drop you off and take my time getting there. If it takes more than an hour for you to convince them, well, I'll call you before I go in."

Her fingers grew tighter on his arm. He covered her hand with his. He didn't want this either.

"Okay."

He looked at her as he paused for a turn. "I'll bet you were something in court."

Her smile was a bit shaky. "I never really got the chance to find out."

"Well, now you do." It wasn't a court with a judge, but she'd be arguing their case. "My money is on you."

Her fingers squeezed his arm once more and then withdrew. His arm felt cold where her touch had been. He wanted to say something, but nothing in his training had prepared him for this.

THE POLICE WEREN'T AS skeptical as Maddie had expected. Maybe Robbie G. Lee had seeded the ground for them. Whatever the reason, they listened to her.

"You don't actually know there is a threat?"

"Quinn is certain. She didn't sound like herself." She glanced at the clock. They didn't know Quinn hadn't gone inside yet. She bet they'd get moving if they knew that, which was why she hadn't told them.

She had to let him go inside. Even if the thought of it made her feel like she might die, too.

"We've been getting interesting information on Mr. Ellery."

It might be a good thing she was talking directly to the chief of police. He opened a folder on his desk and pretended to read a sheet of paper.

"Former SEAL. Good record. Separated in 2020." He glanced up but didn't ask the question.

An officer came in and handed him something. He read it and then looked up.

"Now this is interesting. Our corpse is not James Carver. He visited the local dentist while he was here in 1963 and his X-rays don't match."

"That is interesting," Maddie said. It felt like the clock's ticking filled the space around her, but it wasn't that kind of clock. It was all in her head. Did that mean James Carver was still alive? "Any idea yet who it is?"

"Well, as you probably already know, Ms. *Baker*."

The slight emphasis on her last name wasn't needed. The Baker name always proceeded her.

"Identification of corpses that old take time. We're going through missing persons cases now and trying to find a match."

His fingers tapped on the top of the desk, a jazz rhythm. Maddie had to resist the impulse to tap her feet in time.

"That Miss Ashbourne is a bit of a character, but I'd hate to see anything happen to her. Did Mr. Ellery tell you what he wanted us to do?"

"He wouldn't try to tell you your job," Maddie said evenly.

"Now I'm glad to hear that."

"What are you going to do?" Did he believe her?

"I might have a little trouble with your story if it weren't for that bomb a few days ago. That was interesting, too." He rose to his feet, but didn't leave. Instead, he looked down at her. "I'm waiting for the Parish SWAT team to get ready. You familiar enough with the interior of the house to help with the briefing?"

"Yes."

"Wait here. It won't be long."

When she was alone, she looked at her watch. He'd be heading inside soon. What would happen then? Was Gammie okay? Her cellphone buzzed. It was Gemma.

"I'm sending you what I found," she said without too much preliminary talking.

She must be at work.

"Thanks, Gemma. Like I said, I owe you."

She had to pull it up on her phone. It took her longer. Gemma was awesome. She'd found both men and run them through aging software. She studied all four images carefully, then read through what information Gemma had found to go with them.

Leroy had left Beauville soon after Etta Mae's death. He'd gone into the military and then gone off the grid. She frowned. Had she seen a photo of Quinn's Sol? Could he be Leroy Washington? But if he was, why had he gone off the grid? And did that remove the link between her and Sol? But where did Gammie fit into the story if it wasn't about Etta Mae's murder?

Were they chasing two completely different stories with two different endings? Or was it two stories converging—colliding— after so many years?

The police chief came back with a commander rigged out in full SWAT gear.

She rose. "I'd like to come with you."

The police chief started to shake his head.

"I won't do anything or get in the way. I just need to be there," she said.

The chief glanced at the commander who finally nodded.

"You give me any trouble, I'll arrest you."

"She's a lawyer," the chief said.

"I won't do anything. I'm also the daughter of a cop."

The chief nodded. "That's true. She's a Baker out of New Orleans."

That got her a long, thoughtful look. He gave a short nod. "Let's brief and then we'll roll."

QUINN SAT for several minutes in the drive, studying the front of the house. It looked just like it always did, other than the crime scene tape around the bombed out office.

No sign of anyone at the windows. Another indication Gammie wasn't acting willingly. She heard a car. She was up and looking out. Then she'd open the door and smile so big it should have ruined her old skin. But it didn't. She lit up when family came to call.

Was she still alive in there?

If she wasn't, well, then he wouldn't have to hold back. If she was okay? Then they'd talk.

He climbed out and headed toward the front door. It was out of character. Everyone used the back door at Gammie's, except the uppity types.

He climbed the steps, crossed the porch, and knocked lightly on the door. He heard Gammie call for him to come in. He turned the knob and pushed the door open.

He heard the click of a bullet being chambered.

QUINN'S TRUCK was in the driveway, but there was no sign of him as the police car she rode in pulled to a stop just down the street from the house.

The cop turned, but before he could speak, she said, "I'll just wait here."

The SWAT van was screened from the house by trees and bushes. The team rolled out with quiet efficiency and melted into the yards of the nearby houses.

She couldn't see their commander or the chief. Based on what she'd learned from her brother, they'd be inside the van managing tactical, waiting for the team to get into position.

She noticed two guys moving below the level of the windows around the front of Gammie's house. They crawled up onto the porch and in a few minutes, she saw a fiber optic camera moving slowly in front of the window.

She wished she was in the van with them, wished she could see what they saw.

Her phone buzzed and she jumped, her heart thumping like a drum. She pulled it out and looked at the screen.

It was Quinn.

"Hello?"

"Ms. Baker?"

"Yes."

"Someone here wants to talk to you."

"Okay." Maddie shifted, looking behind her.

"This M. Baker?"

It wasn't the unknown cop's voice. She felt the certainty of this to her toes.

"Yes."

"I want an address. The address of that author."

And here it was.

"Why?" Maddie felt the need to stall.

"That's my business."

The voice was male with a hint of Cajun in the way he spoke.

"It would be unfortunate if something were to happen to Ms. Ashbourne here and her grandson."

"How do I know you won't hurt them if I do tell you? I presume they've seen you. I tell you what you want to know. You hurt them, then go hurt my author."

"I don't want to hurt anyone."

"I don't suppose you do," Maddie said. She went with her gut but crossed her fingers. "I'm guessing you haven't hurt anyone since Etta Mae—until now. What went wrong, James?"

"I don't know what you're talking about. I'm not..."

"You were married. You were leaving. Going somewhere the law wouldn't interfere. North, I suppose. To get away from the Jim Crow laws. But something went wrong. It was probably an accident. You wouldn't hurt her on purpose. You loved her."

Silence.

"You argued about Leroy Washington." She was crawling out

on a limb now. She'd just lost him if she were wrong about this. She softened her tone. "I expect it was hard to be so in love and not be able to talk to anyone about it. To pretend. Even harder for Etta Mae to pretend that Leroy was her boyfriend so no one would suspect."

Still more silence.

"And then you started to wonder. What if she's not pretending? What if it is Leroy she loves. It's easier for her. Her family would like that better. It's hard to go against your family."

Trust her, boy, did she know about that.

"And you were willing to give up your family for her. How could she be afraid? How could she let you down?"

"It wasn't Leroy!" His voice rose in anger and Maddie bit her lip.

"You heard gossip about Walter." She hesitated. "I never met him, so I don't know much about it except what Gammie told me. People say things that aren't true all the time. And they are both gone. What are you afraid of, James?"

"I thought it was over and done with," he said now, his voice slurred almost. "And then I got the letter..."

"Letter?"

"I got a letter that said that author was going to write a book about it. At first, I wasn't worried, but then...I came back, just to make sure. And I heard..."

"People talking about Gammie and her murder. Only it wasn't her murder to talk about. It was yours."

"Don't move!" The shout made her flinch back from the phone.

"James!" Maddie said his name with as much authority as she could manage. "I need you to focus."

In the background, she heard Gammie speaking.

"I'm getting very tired of this, James. I'm sure your mama taught you better than this."

It might not have been the best idea to mention his mother.

"No, ma'am I mean yes, ma'am. Don't bring my mama into this. She did her best."

"I'm sure she did."

His mother had to be gone. Surely.

Maddie saw two of the SWAT team positioned on either side of the door. The three of them must be in the front room. It looked to her like SWAT was getting ready to go in.

"James," Maddie tried to get his attention. "You need to put the gun down."

This silence was a listening one.

"The cops are outside, aren't they?"

Maddie didn't like the tone of his voice. Suicide by cop was a real thing. But Gammie and Quinn were also in the line of fire.

The line went dead.

Quinn felt and saw Carver unraveling. He'd heard some of what Maddie said, and then heard Carver say the police were outside. He also saw his attention waver away from Gammie.

He moved, throwing himself between Carver and Gammie, and then twisting toward Carver to take him down.

Dang, wooden floors were hard.

His hands were around Carver's gun hand as he tried to get it pointed toward him or possibly Gammie. He was old, almost as old as Gammie, but he had a wiry strength fueled by panic and rage.

Quinn could hold him but that was about all.

He slammed Carver's arm against the floor and the gun flew out of sight.

Freed from that constraint, he got Carver subdued, their faces inches from each other.

"Why did you kill Sol?"

Carver blinked up at him, the rage slowly dying from his gaze.

"Sol? Who's that?"

"My neighbor," with great reluctance, Quinn said the name. "Why did you kill him?"

"I didn't. Why would I do that?"

And looking down at Carver, with all the events of the past few days playing inside his head, he knew Carver was telling the truth.

He hadn't killed Sol. And he certainly hadn't master-minded any of the events that had thrown them into so much of a tangle. He was no master and he barely had a mind, in Quinn's opinion.

The front door burst open, SWAT team members arriving there and from the back.

Quinn released Carver to their care and went to Gammie.

"Are you all right?"

"I don't know what you were thinking walking in here after I warned you off. To what? Rescue an old woman who should know better than to stir up the past."

He grinned tiredly as her scolding washed over him.

He bent and kissed the top of her head. "I love you, too."

She mock slapped him, her hand stopping at contact and turning into a pat. But her gaze was serious, too. "If he didn't kill your friend, then who did?"

Before he could tell her he didn't know, a stir at the door had him turning, half in alarm. Alarm that faded as soon as he saw who stood there.

"Quinn." She half stepped forward, then seemed to stop herself. "You're alright. You're both alright?"

He took a half step toward her and stopped. "We're good. We're both good. You did good."

Gammie humphed behind him. "You always did have a way with words."

She didn't say the rest, to his relief. *A lousy way.*

"Gammie," Maddie said, "Why aren't you in New Orleans?"

"I got a message that I thought was from Quinn..." She stopped, playing old lady now, with her hands fluttering.

"You two don't have a safe word?" Maddie shook her head.

"We'll get to work on that," Quinn said.

"You could at least give the girl a hug or something," Gammie hissed.

Well, she wasn't wrong about that.

Somehow, he found himself holding her close, her hair brushing his face, and her soft scent filling his nostrils. He had to restrain himself from tightening his hold. He lightly rested his cheek against the bright fall of hair.

"It's not over, you know," he said.

He felt her sigh in his soul.

"No, it's not over."

13

"I think we need to take another look at your other two murders," Quinn said, finally breaking the silence that had fallen since the cops had cleared out.

Gammie had gone into her room to catch her breath, leaving Maddie and Quinn alone in the kitchen.

No one had said anything when she fixed them food, rooting around in the kitchen as if she lived there. They'd eaten, had cold drinks, and Quinn had cleaned up.

The table was small enough that their knees had to bump together. It felt good to have any point of contact after the stress of the last couple of hours.

"Whether you ever write the books, it is possible that one or both killers are still out there," he added.

"Yeah." Maddie sighed. Without her laptop, all she had to work with was the picture she'd taken of the whiteboard before they left *The Reel Escape.*

She pulled it up on her phone, then slid her chair next to Quinn's so they could both look at the image.

She zoomed in on the Darrow case first because the crime

had been identified. In the Merrick case, the industrial espionage had just been the suspected motive.

"So, there were four suspects at the time," Quinn said, peering at the screen of her phone.

She enlarged the image to where they'd written down the suspects.

"I guess you can call them that. Gladys Montgomery, the victim's friend and neighbor."

"Mrs. Darrow was blackmailing her own friend?"

Maddie recalled he'd been just as incredulous the last time they'd covered this.

"According to her daughter, money was tight after her husband died."

"And the blackmail was that Gladys cheated to become the local beauty queen?"

"Apparently." Maddie moved the image to the next suspect. "Marty Harrington was the mailman, and she found out he was stealing mail. Stupid stuff, but it was stealing. He's deceased."

"So, three suspects?"

"Two actually," Maddie said. "Scooter Higgins is also dead."

"He was the Peeping Tom handyman."

"Who is our live, second suspect?"

"That would be Bernice Walker."

"Oh, yeah," Quinn grinned. "The church secretary with the gambling problem."

"To be fair, she put the money back when she won," Maddie pointed out, meeting his grin with one of her own.

"But she didn't win that often."

"No."

Quinn frowned down at the image. "None of them seem like the kind of wily planner of our current problem."

Our. Maddie felt warmth at the words. Technically, it was her problem.

"No," she said. "The Merrick case is cloudier. They suspected industrial espionage but couldn't prove it because, presumably, Merrick interrupted the thief or something. In any case, if something was stolen, it was never used."

Quinn's frown deepened. "That anyone knows, it was never used," he pointed out.

"That's true, I guess. The company had a government contract, so what they did wasn't known."

"How come his partner isn't on our list of suspects?" Quinn asked. "He basically got the business afterwards, didn't he?"

"Cast-iron alibi," Maddie said. "He was in the hospital having surgery on his knee."

"So, he couldn't even hobble out to kill." Quinn sounded disappointed.

"The main suspect was Paul Palfrey. A rival businessman who didn't get the government contract that Merrick bid for." Maddie gave a shiver. "His picture gave me the creeps just looking at it, but if he did kill Merrick..."

"And the other two suspects were a disgruntled former employee and a somewhat shady nephew."

"Yeah," Maddie rubbed her face.

"I'll have to admit that Palfrey seems like the most likely. How old is he?"

"He'd have to be in his sixties, late sixties maybe?" She really wished she had her laptop. She switched to the ChatGPT app and asked it how old he was. She tried not to play favorites between it and Grok. If they eventually took over the world, she wanted to be friends with both of them. "Okay, he's seventy-one."

"Our possibly bogus cop looked younger than that to me," Quinn said.

Maddie's only real experience with seventy and older was

Zach. She pulled up the footage and watched it, then zoomed in on his hands.

"Definitely not that old," Maddie said, showing the frozen image of the hands to him.

She noted, with some amusement, that he studied his own hands, then the image again.

"No, but older than me, I'd guess."

She wanted to put her hand over his, but she didn't. She set the phone down and thought about their suspects and what they could do about it.

"We need to draw him out," Maddie said, finally. She didn't like saying it. It felt like an iffy TV plot. Setting a trap for bad guys didn't go that well when it flowed from a script. But she couldn't think of any way to get the guy to stop toying with them.

If he was their guy, if he'd killed Sol, then he wasn't going to just stop and slither away.

Quinn shot her a look, but didn't agree or disagree.

"We need some research about the people related to this case, to our suspects. Possibly even the dead ones."

"Gemma?"

"Gemma," he agreed.

To QUINN'S SURPRISE, Gammie raised no objections when he told her they needed to leave. He may have implied that they'd done all they could because she said, "I hope you aren't going to let that little gal get away. I like her."

"I like her, too," he admitted. "And I don't plan to let her get away."

Gammie looked satisfied. "You should sell that house and move back to Beauville. Settle down."

"I'll think on it," he told her, like he always did. He liked

Plonkville, but it was true it wouldn't be the same without his cranky neighbor.

Maddie gave Gammie a careful hug before they left.

"I didn't want to break her," she explained as they walked to his truck. Gemma had just clambered into the passenger seat when her cellphone vibrated.

She pulled it out and looked at the screen. It was *the* number.

"Hello?"

"Ms. Baker?"

It was him, the same voice. She looked at Quinn and waved her phone. She put it on speaker.

"Yes, this is Ms. Baker."

"It's probably time we met face to face."

~

"I DON'T THINK this guy is who we think he is," Maddie told Quinn, as he headed them back to the courthouse, "if he wants to meet us there."

"He didn't say what he wanted?" Quinn asked, mostly so he'd stop thinking and just drive.

"*A matter of importance,*" Maddie said. "That's all he said before he hung up on me."

She sounded annoyed and he didn't blame her. Most of it, he decided now, had just been annoyances. The woman in the bathroom with the gun was a bit more than annoying, but most of what had happened seemed almost designed to keep them on the hop, spinning and looking in multiple directions.

"It's not very focused, is it?" he said now.

"I definitely have the feeling someone wants us looking in so many directions, we can't see the forest for the trees." She sighed. "I still need to figure out who did it in my book in progress."

Quinn stiffened slightly. "Does anyone else know you don't know that yet?"

Maddie twisted to look at him. "Helen knows it's not who I originally thought it was."

"Helen. The only one who could have spilled the other cases," Quinn pointed out. They'd said multiple times that Maddie should call and talk to her and then something happened to send them in a different direction. "The book you're working on, it's not out there yet? I mean there's no publicity yet on it?"

"Promo is focused on my current release. Once I turn it in, they'll start to ramp things up." She rubbed her head. "If I made my deadline, which is in serious jeopardy right now." She hitched a breath. "Could that be what this is all about? But then, how could making me twist in the wind affect my author? They don't know..."

"You're sure they don't?"

Maddie was silent for a while. "I suppose if someone really dug down, like a Gemma-like person, they might realize my Fitz-D doesn't exist. But if they knew, then why kill your Fitz-D?"

"To smoke you out?" Quinn tried to think of other reasons for Sol to die and just couldn't, even with his secret identity. He looked up. "There's the courthouse and I'm pretty sure that's our guy waiting in front."

They pulled in and got out, walking over to meet him. They hadn't had a clear view of the man's face, but his gimme cap was the same.

"M. Baker," the man said, walking to meet them.

"Yes. You don't look like a Plonkville cop," Maddie said.

"Well, I'm not. I just needed to give you this."

He held out an envelope. Legal-sized, Quinn noted. Maddie hesitated for a second before accepting it.

"I'm being served?"

"That's right, ma'am. You're hard to find, but I don't give up." He tipped his hat and strolled off, whistling.

"Served?" Quinn asked as Maddie opened the envelope and pulled out what was clearly a legal document. He waited while she read it.

"It's actually an order for me and my client to present ourselves in court for a preliminary hearing."

"About what?"

"The legalese is impressive," Maddie said, "but the gist is that they want to litigate my upcoming projects prior to publication."

She studied the sheets again.

"Some legal gymnastics here. This lawyer deserves a gold medal in obfuscation."

"Who is the lawyer?"

"Her name is Calder," Maddie said. "Which is definitely interesting. That's the name of the boyfriend. But the judge is also interesting." She looked up and met his gaze. "His name is Haverly."

"Calder and Haverly." Quinn said. "Both names from the book you're working on right now."

"It could be a coincidence."

She didn't sound convinced. He wasn't either.

"Where's the hearing?" he asked. Maybe it wasn't a coincidence. "And when is it?"

Maddie went back to the sheets. "Well, well. It's in the little town where the murder happened. Centerton, Mississippi. And the hearing is tomorrow. That guy cut it pretty close to the wire."

"Good thing Mississippi is so close."

She looked up again, this time startled.

"I'm coming with you."

Her smile curled his toes. And the best part, he didn't care. Neither did his toes.

14

I t hadn't been easy to get her ducks in a row. Maddie was amazed to find them walking into yet another courthouse in time for their hearing.

She'd visited Centerton doing research for the book, but she hadn't advertised her reasons for being there. Mostly she'd walked around the town, visited the sites key to the story and soaked up the ambience.

"You seem to be drawn to small town murders," Quinn murmured under his breath.

Was she? She did a quick mental assessment and realized, with surprise, that he was correct.

In the corridor outside the courtroom, Maddie jerked to a halt.

"Helen?" Her voice echoed some from the modestly soaring ceiling.

The older woman strode over to meet her, both relief and curiosity in her gaze, which flickered to Quinn for a long moment before returning to Maddie.

"Is this..."

"No," Maddie said.

Relief turned to alarm.

"Is he coming then? Already here?"

"What are you doing here?" Maddie said.

"I got served, too."

Maddie glanced at her watch. They didn't have much time. She took Helen's arm and led her over to a bench in a corner that looked like it might be quiet.

Quinn followed them, but Maddie noticed he'd gone all watchful again. That was good. She needed someone to do that while she tried to get to the bottom of Helen's involvement.

"How did they find out what I was writing, Helen?"

"I have no idea," Helen began.

Maddie raised her eyebrows. "Someone knows about my other possible projects, too, not just the Haverly project. What's going on?"

Helen's gaze shifted away. "What you do is so interesting project, Maddie, I might have mentioned them to one or two people in passing."

"Helen," Maddie's tone brought her gaze back. "Someone has been sending anonymous letters to people in all the cases on that list I gave you two years ago."

Helen's eyes widened.

"And now someone is trying to stop a work in progress that no one but you and I should know about."

"And the author."

"And the author. Do you really think he's the one who talked? Seriously?"

"Well, I can't know that. I've never met him." She sounded snappish now.

"The lawyer and the judge both have names related to the Haverly case. Surely you noticed that?"

"Well, I didn't! I was so shocked to get served and then I had to move a bunch of meetings and my personal schedule around at the last minute. Thankfully, Roger is very under-standing."

"Roger?" Maddie wasn't sure why she locked onto the name. Instincts maybe.

"My," Helen gave an artificial laugh, "at my age it sounds so silly to say I have a boyfriend, but I guess that's what he is." Her gaze flickered to Quinn again.

"Roger who?"

"Roger Smith."

Well, that didn't sound fake at all.

"Is he one of the people you told in passing?"

Helen shifted uncomfortably and looked at her watch. "They'll be waiting for us."

"We have sixty seconds. Was he?"

"I might have mentioned them to him, but he'd have no real reason to be interested. He was just being supportive of my work. He's the nicest man, Maddie. So thoughtful. Not like a man at all!"

"Did he come with you?" Maddie resisted the urge to glance around.

"Of course not. He's got his own affairs to look after, but he did take me to the airport. Neither of my other husbands ever did that without complaining. You just don't know what it's like, Maddie."

Now there was a pleading note in Helen's voice. Maddie wanted to sigh and shake her head. She didn't.

She was glad that this courthouse was so small they didn't screen for weapons when you entered.

QUINN FOLLOWED Maddie and Helen into the courtroom. It was small, but then so was the town that built it.

He took a seat in the back. There was a woman at one table. Selena Calder, he guessed. One of the things Maddie had done was get united with her laptop and do a deep dive on both the lawyer and the judge.

Selena Calder was the daughter of the man Maddie suspected of committing the murder. Her father, still considered by one and all as a good man, had gone on to do a lot of good works, including efforts in helping victims of crimes.

He did seem like an unlikely murderer, Quinn had to admit.

The judge was related to the cold-hearted husband, Darin Haverly. It felt like they'd found their intersection point, but they still didn't know from which direction the threat would come.

What was the point of bringing Maddie, the author, and Helen here? Was it a last attempt—a law abiding one—to stop the publication of the story? Or something more sinister?

Maddie was going to have to out herself if the judge insisted. She was a lawyer, and it was going to come out anyway. But how much risk was she incurring by doing it here?

So, he sat in the back, his gaze monitoring everyone coming in and going out.

The judge hadn't entered yet, but the usual staff were milling around, all three of them. One approached Maddie when she took her place at the opposing counsel table.

The lawyer, Selena Calder, gave her a hard look, then walked over. They exchanged a few words, shook hands, and then Calder went back to her spot.

There was a stir and then the room was called to order. Everyone rose for the judge to enter.

He was a thin, dyspeptic looking man whose frown appeared to be permanent. He called the room to order, and the formalities commenced as the case number was called out.

Maddie rose and faced him, no sign of tension in her shoulders that Quinn could see.

The judge put on a pair of reading glasses and studied the paperwork.

"Is this man, Fitz-Dankworthington present?"

"Yes, and no, your honor," Maddie said.

The judge took off the glasses to bring the full force of his scowl to bear on her.

"I have power of attorney to act..."

The judge cut her off. "Are you trying for a contempt of court citation, young lady?"

"No, your honor."

"Then explain to me how he is here and yet not here?"

Quinn saw Maddie's shoulders rise and fall in a sigh.

"Your honor, S.C. Fitz-Dankworthington is a pseudonym adopted by the author to protect her privacy."

"You're telling me this Fitz-whatever is a woman?"

"Yes, your honor."

"I don't care. I want her in this courtroom now."

"She is in your courtroom, your honor."

The judge scanned the room. "Then she needs to stand up and come forward."

"She is standing up, your honor. I'm the author S. C. Fitz-Dankworthington."

There was a slight rustle as her words settled over the sparsely filled room. Helen gasped.

"Really, Maddie..."

The judge used his gavel with a certain relish.

"Indeed," he said.

"I'm also a lawyer, your honor. I've been reading this," she hesitated, "case. It is quite remarkable. I can't help but wonder if its sole purpose was to out the author."

The judge picked up what Quinn presumed was the legal document behind their summons here and read it in what felt like a deliberately slow manner. Then he looked at Calder.

"Well, Ms. Calder? Do you have anything to say?"

Calder scrambled to her feet. "Your honor, that is an outrageous accusation."

"But nevertheless, a true one, is it not? What else do you hope to achieve? This request for a *remedy,*" the judge almost spat the words out, "is an insult to me, as well as the plaintiff."

"Your...honor?"

"I allowed this hearing because I was curious. And let's face it, most of my cases are boring. But you've found out what you wanted to know. There's the author. Now what, Ms. Calder?"

"Well, we want her to be enjoined from writing a book about my client."

The judge studied her for a length of time that would have made Quinn nervous.

"You do realize what country this is, Ms. Calder? People write books that annoy other people all the time." His gaze swiveled suddenly back to Maddie.

"Is this book finished?"

"No, your honor."

"So, your client doesn't even know what the book is going to say, Ms. Calder? They just want it stopped?"

"The original case was painful, your honor, and distressful for my client."

"I remember," he said, dryly.

Did the old boy actually have a sense of humor?

"Yes, your honor."

"Who is your client, Ms. Calder?"

"It's in the paperwork..."

"Ms. Baker had to say she was the author in this court. I think you can name your client."

"My father, your honor." Were her teeth gritted, Quinn wondered. "Ephram Calder."

"There have been television episodes about the case," the

judge pointed out. "And most people know about Eph's involvement."

"Yes, your honor, but Mr...the author has a high profile with a potentially wider audience. The damage to my client..."

"Your father," the judge put in.

"...could be substantially higher."

"What do you have to say to that, Ms. Baker?"

Maddie didn't speak immediately, which impressed Quinn. He could see some of her profile as she quietly regarded the judge.

"What you seem to be asking, your honor, is why do I write books about old, unsolved murders?"

Now it was the judge's turn to look thoughtful.

"I suppose I am."

"My first book was, quite honestly, an exercise in working through a theory after I saw a television episode about it. I," Maddie raised her hands to make air quotes, "solved it in my head and on paper. It was a puzzle and my brain likes puzzles."

She hesitated, then stepped out in front of the judge. "But there was also a sense of vindication for the victim. These courts are about justice. And no, the book didn't deliver justice for that victim. Everyone involved was already dead. But," she half shrugged, "it felt good to know that her story was told, her killer identified, even if it was just in a book."

The judge nodded.

"Justice. But as you point out, it's a book, not a court of law."

"No, your honor, and I never expect any real legal justice from one of my books. I haven't the power to exact justice but there is power in a story, in telling someone's story so that they get heard."

"And a lot of money," Ms. Calder interjected. "Readers love crime stories, don't they, Ms. Baker?"

Maddie turned to face her. "They do. I'm one of them. But

the readers of crime and mystery stories are drawn to them because of the justice aspect. Books, both fiction and nonfiction, help us make sense of a world that doesn't often make sense to us." She swung back to face the judge. "Sometimes words are all we have to fight back, to restore a kind of order."

She suddenly swung back to face Calder.

"Aren't you getting paid by your client today?"

Calder actually took a step back. "Of course?"

"So, you're making money off of someone else's misery? But that's okay because...?"

"It's my job!"

"And writing books is my job. The fact that I make money from it isn't really relevant. The essential question here is my right to do it?" She faced the judge again.

"That's true, Ms. Baker. Thank you for not pointing out that I also make money from others' misery."

The old boy did have a sense of humor. It was annoying he'd made them come all this way so he could exercise it, but judges lived by their own rules.

The judge lifted his gavel. "The injunctive relief is refused. I would suggest, Ms. Calder, that going forward, you rely more on the law and less on hyperbole."

Maddie swung around, her eyes gleaming with humor, then they widened as the door next to him swung open.

Quinn turned and saw the gun first. Then the masked guy holding it.

It felt like everything switched to slow motion mode, as Maddie dove for the floor, her weapon in her hand without even realizing she'd reached for it.

She crawled forward to the barrier that separated the seating from the official proceedings, trying to flatten herself even more as bullets ripped through the space where she'd been standing.

The shooting stopped as abruptly as it had begun, to be replaced with the sounds of a scuffle.

Maddie glanced toward Ms. Calder. She lay in a crumpled heap on the floor across from her.

Maddie belly crawled toward her, found her wrist, found a pulse. She used Calder's scarf to bind up a wound, then got cautiously to her knees.

She couldn't see Quinn, but she heard bodies banging into the wooden seats.

"Helen?" She'd almost forgotten Helen was there during her verbal sparring with the judge.

"Maddie?" Her voice quavered. "Are you all right?"

"I'm fine. Are you all right?"

"Well, mostly. My body isn't used to diving under seats."

That's why Maddie liked her, she remembered now. A sense of humor when she wasn't doing evil editor.

"Stay down."

Maddie saw deputies run in and the court guard trying to get close to the fighting men. There was a thump and then silence.

She saw Quinn stand up, his arms raised to face the deputies.

"He's out cold," Quinn said.

The deputies didn't lower their weapons. The judge got up from behind his bench and looked with annoyance at the bullet holes in the walls.

"He was in the courtroom," the judge snapped. "It's the other one that started the shooting."

Quinn stepped aside, so the deputies could reach the assailant.

"I think I knocked him out," Quinn said. "He quit fighting me."

"Good," the judge said approvingly. He glanced at his clerk. "Did you call 911?"

"Yes, sir," she gasped from her spot on the floor.

One of the two deputies dragged the prone figure out from between the benches into the center aisle. His face was covered.

Maddie vaguely remembered noticing that as she made her own painful dive to the deck.

The other deputy kept him covered while the mask was removed.

"Roger!" Helen gasped.

"So, WHO IS HE REALLY?" Quinn asked, as they waited in the judge's antechamber for the machinations of the law to finish.

Maddie shook her head, but the judge chose that moment to enter. He closed the door.

"That was unfortunate," he said.

"Yes," Maddie said doubtfully.

"I have you to thank, young man. Quick thinking."

"He's a former SEAL," Maddie offered, as Quinn accepted the handshake.

"Aw." The judge went and sat down. "I recognized him, of course. He's Selena Calder's brother. I thought he lived in New York. What I don't understand is why?"

"I might know," Maddie said.

"If you're worried about a conflict of interest, he tried to shoot me, too," the judge pointed out dryly.

"Right. When I began working on the book, I believed the husband was the killer and was trying to work out how to break his alibi." Maddie gave a wry grin. "But more and more, I became convinced that it was Ephram Calder who was actually the killer."

"Ah," the judge said. "Ephram actually did quite well out of being the broken-hearted lover, but what proof do you have to offer?"

"That's the thing, your honor, I never have proof, just a theory. I've been struggling with finishing the book because of the legal ramifications."

The judge actually chuckled. "Well, you probably won't have to worry about that now that Eph's son tried to kill you."

"Every cloud has a silver lining," Quinn said, quoting Gammie.

This time the judge laughed.

15

There was a painful scene with Helen to get through. She and Quinn drove her back to the airport to catch her flight back to New York.

"I should have known he was too good to be true," Helen said, finally, as she stood outside as Quinn unloaded her bag.

It was, Maddie thought, kind of obvious. Men were just guys, human, flawed—she glanced at Quinn—and amazing at the same time. They were good in their lane.

"Well, I finally found out."

It didn't surprise Maddie that Helen now switched to business.

"You've been very sly about this whole thing."

"It was hard to stop, once it started and even my family didn't know."

That appeared to make Helen feel better.

"You need to meet your deadline," she said, grabbed her bag and headed for the door.

"She'll be alright," Maddie said to Quinn.

"And you?" Quinn asked, leaning against the side of his truck, his expression enigmatic.

"Well, I don't seem to have any more problems," Maddie said, feeling her heart clench at the thought. He'd stayed for the problems. Now what?

"I have a big one," Quinn said. He straightened, and gently grasped her shoulders.

"Oh?" Her heart turned from clenching to thumping.

"What excuse do I have to stay in your life?"

Maddie's lips twitched a little. "Do you need an excuse? We could do something crazy. Instead of dodging bullets and crazy people, we could...date?"

"I like that idea." He drew her a little closer, so she had to tip her head back to see him. "But you need to understand it will be dating with intent."

"Intent?"

"Since you're a lawyer, I thought I ought to use a legal word for wanting to stay in your life for a very long time."

"I am happy to agree to your terms." Her heart now thumped so loud she almost couldn't hear her own words.

"Then we should seal the deal." He pulled her against him. "I've been wanting to do this since I walked into that office and saw you sitting there all Della Street prim."

And then he kissed her.

With intent.

THANK you for reading *Gumbo Ya-Ya Exit*! I hope you enjoyed it! The next book in the series will be arriving in 2026! In the meantime, grab this exclusive followup scene as Quinn and Maddie meet the folks.

To find out about all my releases, be sure to sign up for my New Release eZine and get a free eBook by visiting my website.

If you enjoyed this book, I hope you'll consider leaving a review. It's not just because I'm needy (even though I try not to be!). Reviews help other readers decide which books to buy. :-)

ALSO BY PAULINE BAIRD JONES

Romantic Suspense

The Big Uneasy Series:

Relatively Risky (1)

Dead Spaces (2.0)

Louisiana Lagniappe (3.0)

Worry Beads (4.0)

Fais Do Do Die (5.0)

Beaucoup Fracas (6.0)

Pirogue Wipe Out (7.0)

Bourre Brouhaha (8.0)

Soc Au' Lait Stiff (9.0)

Gumbo Ya-Ya Exit (10.0)

Family Treed (A Big Uneasy Short Story)

The Family Way (A Big Uneasy Short Story)

Guess Who's Coming To Christmas: The Wedding Edition (A Big Uneasy Short Story)

The Big Uneasy Bundle

An Uneasy Collection: The Shorts

Lonesome Lawmen Series:

The Last Enemy

Byte Me

Missing You

Lonesome Mama (Bonus short story)

(The *Lonesome Lawmen* is also available as a digital bundle)

Do Wah Diddy Die

The Spy Who Kissed Me

Perilously Fun Fiction Bundle (includes *The Spy Who Kissed Me* and *Do Wah Diddy Die*. Bonus: *Do Wah Diddy Delete Short Story Collection*)

Dangerous Dance

A Dangerous Duet - 2020

Science Fiction Romance/Paranormal

Project Enterprise: The Cyborg Chronicles (Coming in 2023!)

Cyborg's Revenge: The Cyborg Chronicles Book 1

Cosmic Boom: The Cyborg Chronicles Book 2

CabeX: The Cyborg Chronicles Book 3

AzumC: The Cyborg Chronicles Book 4

MircoP: The Cyborg Chronicles Book 5

ScytheQ: The Cyborg Chronicles 6

OmnitronW: The Cyborg Chronicles 7

TalusH: The Cyborg Chronicles 8

Project Universe Series:

The Key (book 1)

Girl Gone Nova (book 2)

Tangled in Time (book 3)

Steamrolled (book 4)

Kicking Ashe (book 5)

The Reboot Books of Project Enterprise

Short Story Collections

Project Enterprise: The Short Stories

Do Wah Diddy Delete

Let's Fall in Love

The Real Dragon and other short stories

ABOUT THE AUTHOR

Award-winning, *USA Today* Bestselling author Pauline never liked reality, so she writes books. She likes to wander among the genres, rampaging like Godzilla, because she does love peril mixed in her romance.

To find out more about Pauline or her books:
http://paulinebjones.com